Tread Softly, Nurse Scott!

Tread Softly, Nurse Scott!

Marilyn Ross

THORNDIKE
CHIVERS

This Large Print edition is published by Thorndike Press®, Waterville, Maine USA and by BBC Audiobooks Ltd, Bath, England.

Published in 2006 in the U.S. by arrangement with Maureen Moran Agency.

Published in 2006 in the U.K. by arrangement with the author.

U.S. Hardcover   0-7862-8787-X (Candlelight)
U.K. Hardcover 10: 1 4056 3874 5   (Chivers Large Print)
U.K. Hardcover 13: 978 1 405 63874 6
U.K. Softcover 10: 1 4056 3875 3   (Camden Large Print)
U.K. Softcover 13: 978 1 405 63875 3

The text of this Large Print edition is unabridged. Other aspects of the book may vary from the original edition.

Set in 16 pt. Plantin by Al Chase.

Printed in the United States on permanent paper.

British Library Cataloguing-in-Publication Data available

Library of Congress Cataloging-in-Publication Data
Ross, Marilyn, 1912–
    Tread softly, Nurse Scott / by Marilyn Ross.
        p. cm. — (Thorndike Press large print Candlelight)
    ISBN 0-7862-8787-X (lg. print : hc : alk. paper)
    1. Nurses — Fiction. I. Title. II. Series: Thorndike Press large print Candlelight series.
    PR9199.3.R5996T73 2006
    813'.54—dc22
                                                2006009828

Tread Softly, Nurse Scott!

CHAPTER ONE

For just a fraction of a second Nurse Judy Scott let her eyes wander to the big clock over the double doors of the operating room. She saw they had been there more than an hour and at once she realized why she had suddenly gotten this uneasy feeling. Dr. Holland was taking too long!

"Rib spreader!" The senior surgeon of Bedford City Hospital sounded his usual assured self.

She passed it to him and he placed it carefully between the fourth and fifth ribs, his skilled hands working swiftly in the old manner. Within the area of the incision the patient's lung rose and fell. She began to lose her touch of nervousness and think everything was going all right. It was just that she had not been called in to act as scrub nurse for so long, and it made her a little on edge.

"Reduce pressure," Dr. Graham Holland said in his crisp almost harsh tone. "Now the lung forceps."

She had them ready. As the old surgeon worked, she saw the slight furrow of his brows, and although his stern, bulldog face was covered by a mask like her own, she could picture the frown that would be on it. Not in the more than two years since she had occasionally been called in to serve as his scrub nurse had she seen him so tense or work so slowly.

Now the assistant surgeon, Dr. Miles Small, began to take an active part as the lung was further exposed. She had seen the X-ray plates and knew what they were looking for — a faint shadow in the root of the lung — a faint shadow that almost certainly indicated a growth; and the growth, a suspected cancer.

Miles Small, tall, slim, elegant in voice and manner, raised his head as he addressed the senior surgeon. "You were right," he said.

"A good guess," Dr. Holland agreed. "But there were all the signs. Easier to predict than tomorrow's weather." His gloved fingers had exposed the undersection of the lung to show the deadly grayish-white of the cancer. It spread across an area nearly an inch in diameter.

"Any other involvement?" Miles Small's question was as much a comment as anything else as he assisted the senior surgeon in his probing.

"Hasn't reached the pericardium," Dr. Holland said as he deftly explored the area. Satisfaction showed in his crisp tone when he followed this with the announcement, "The liver is all right!" He continued his search of the pleura for any other sign that the cancer had spread.

"He may have a chance," Dr. Small said.

The senior surgeon had finished his examination and now he nodded curtly and turned to Judy. "Forceps!"

She gave them to him and was ready with scalpel and scissors when the sharp commands for them followed. Now the old surgeon was more like himself. The team gathered around the operating table worked with a fresh precision. Judy was caught up in the atmosphere of it and all her uneasiness left her.

Even the assisting surgeon, Miles Small, whom Judy often considered too faltering in his approach, stepped in to take his full share of the operation. The second hand of the big clock swept on and soon another half-hour had passed.

As Dr. Holland worked he said, "The closest lymph nodes are involved but beyond that it looks good." He brought the diseased ones out and the tiny beanlike nodes touched by the cancer showed speckles of white on their black surface.

Judy said, "They will go to the lab, won't they, Doctor?"

"Yes, and samples of those nearest the normal ones as well. At least, we can hope they are normal for this poor fellow's sake."

The circulating nurse took the specimens to put in bottles as Dr. Holland continued with surgery. Judy, who normally worked as a day nurse on the surgical floor, recalled the patient when he had entered the hospital about a week before for tests. He was a thin little man of middle-age with a neurotic fear of hospitals and surgery in particular. Since it was almost a foregone conclusion that surgery would be required when Dr. Holland had ordered him in for tests, she had tried to reassure him.

Only the previous afternoon she had stood at the foot of his bed in his private room and said, "You shouldn't worry yourself so about tomorrow morning. Let Dr. Holland and Dr. Small take care of that."

The sallow face of the little man had shown despair. "I wish I could be unconcerned about it, but there's no use pretending. I'm scared!"

Judy smiled at this. "Well, at least you're honest about it! A majority of patients feel the same way but don't admit it. Not even to themselves."

He studied her with interest. "I guess you've handled a lot of patients, Miss Scott?"

"I've been a nurse five years, and spent three of them here in the surgical ward," she told him. As she spoke, it was hard for her to realize it had been that long since she'd graduated. She was twenty-five now, an attractive girl with short auburn hair, big brown eyes under lovely arched brows, and a full generous mouth that often showed a smile but which could compress tightly in quick anger sometimes.

Some of the other nurses joked about her sharp temper outbursts, which were infrequent and usually in what she considered a good cause, but which usually caused some consternation on the part of her unsuspecting victims. Everyone thought she was just a jolly, good-natured young woman until some error caught her attention. Then her temper flamed to match her hair!

Nursing Supervisor Jane Miller had more than once jokingly told her, "Tread softly, Nurse Scott! We have some very sensitive skins among our medical staff."

"The patients need consideration as well," Judy had replied defiantly, "and

11

when I see an error I point it out. Just the same as I want others to check on me."

"Yes, Nurse Scott; I'm certainly frightened bad," the thin man had said from the bed, breaking into her reverie and catching her attention again. "I'm an accountant. Figures are my whole life and I'm stretched out here trying to figure what my odds will be on that operating table tomorrow morning."

She had laughed. "I don't think that will help you much. Dr. Holland doesn't seem worried and he has to do all the work."

"Well, anyway, cross your fingers for good luck for Calvin Ames, Miss Scott." For the first time he managed a wan grin.

"I can't do that; I'll be too busy," she had said. "But I'll be working hard to make it turn out all right."

Now she was and it seemed the outlook was good. She couldn't be sure, but judging from the brief comments she'd heard and what her experienced eyes had seen, she thought Calvin Ames might have an excellent chance of complete recovery. All his fear of surgery had been for nothing.

Dr. Holland asked, "What's the sponge count?" Some of the crispness was gone from his voice. It was just harsh and weary now.

"All accounted for, Doctor," she said.

"Then let's close him up," the senior surgeon said.

Dr. Small removed the rib spreader, and the sewing of the muscles began. Then the clamps were removed and finally, the towels framing the incision. Dr. Holland swabbed the wound with tincture of benzoin. Gauze placed over the long wound was covered with adhesive tape. Calvin Ames was more or less in one piece again and on his way to the recovery room.

"Keep a close watch on this fellow, Dr. Small," the senior surgeon said, "and let me know as soon as we get a lab report."

Miles Small had already taken off his mask. "Yes, Doctor," he said with a nod, a smile on his aristocratic, high-cheekboned face. He was blond with mocking blue eyes and they were bright now as he added, "A good morning's work, Doctor."

"Maybe." Dr. Holland sounded less weary. He glanced at the clock. "Almost noon. I'm past due at St. Mary's." St. Mary's was the city's other hospital. He turned to Judy. "Good to have you on the team again."

She smiled. "I have been eager to work in O.R. more often."

He nodded with a look of satisfaction on

his lined, bulldog countenance. She untied his gown and he slipped it off and gave it to her. Then he handed her his rubber gloves along with his cap and mask. He headed for the dressing room, a commanding figure of a man still, his sturdy old body with not a pound of excess weight carried with quiet dignity. At a distance only the heavy head of iron gray hair betrayed his age.

Yet, as he vanished through the swinging door, Judy felt a kind of sadness sweep through her. The senior surgeon was slowing down. During the first part of this morning's operation it had been too apparent not to notice. It was true that, as he progressed, he had regained much of his old swift adeptness, but for a time it had been Miles Small who had taken the lead. She had never known this to occur before. With a sigh she dismissed her concern by telling herself it could have merely been a bad day for him. Everyone had them.

"I hope you have something more flattering than that smock to wear for the dance tonight," Dr. Small said, coming over to her.

She looked up at the tall young surgeon with a quick smile. "A uniform ought to be just the thing for a Hospital Benefit Dance," she said, a twinkle in her brown eyes.

He laughed. "Perhaps you're right! Wear what you like. Just be ready on time. I'll call for you at nine sharp."

She gave him a despairing glance. "It seems to me you worry more about your social life than you do about your patients."

The young surgeon winked at her. "I have a nice appreciation of what is most important in this world." And with that he went out.

She remained behind to supervise the cleaning up of the operating room, a small smile playing on her pretty face at this comment by Miles Small. She knew he was joking but there were times when she wondered just how seriously he did take his profession.

He was the only son of Brandon Small, an ex-governor of the state, born to wealth and position in the thriving Rhode Island coastal city. He could easily have gone into business, but instead chose a difficult medical career. And he had done well, too. He was gradually coming to be recognized as the successor to the chief surgeon. It was no secret around the hospital that Dr. Holland liked the genial young man as a person and was coaching him to take over when he retired. It was the one decision of Dr. Holland's which left Judy in doubt. She didn't think Miles had an ability to match his bedside manner and also felt he lacked a dedication to his profession.

Yet she liked him in a personal way and had seen a lot of him since coming to Bedford. This was natural as he had once dated her sister Moira. This went back to New York and the days when glamorous, brunette Moira had been a top fashion model there. It was a curious coincidence that through Miles Small she had first met another Bedford young man, Paul Avon, whom she later married.

Paul was also a member of the city's social set and the son of a successful department store owner. Miles, who had been an intern at Bellevue when Moira accepted Paul's proposal and came back to Bedford as his bride, often laughed about the way it had turned out and vowed he intended to marry Judy to even the score.

Judy had lived with an aunt in Boston after the death of her widowed mother and had taken her training there. It was during this time Moira had known success in New York as a model. After Moira came to live in Bedford as Mrs. Paul Avon, she wrote Judy of the serious need for nurses at Bedford City Hospital and also mentioned how much she missed her. As a result, Judy had come to Bedford to work and now lived with Moira and Paul.

The young couple had no children as yet and Paul's father, who was also in real estate, had presented them with a lovely colonial style home in Redmond Acres, one of the most exclusive areas on the outskirts of the city. Judy had a nice large bedroom with her own bath on the second floor and in many ways was ideally happy living with the young couple. The only marring shadow was Paul Avon's jealousy of his lovely wife.

Judy hadn't realized what a problem this was in the beginning although Moira had mentioned it in a casual way. Later she had witnessed several ugly scenes between them when Paul had accused her sister of deliberately flirting with some of the young men in their social circle. Since Miles Small had come back to join the Bedford Hospital staff, he had been the special target for Paul's accusations. For this reason Judy found it difficult dating the young doctor, and she vowed that tonight when he came for her she would try to be ready and waiting. This way she would avoid his coming into the house and meeting Moira or Paul.

The circulating nurse came up to her. "If we hurry it shouldn't take long to finish here."

17

Judy gave her a smile. "It had better not or we'll miss our lunch."

It was twelve-thirty before she reached the cafeteria which was now located in the new wing of the hospital on the ground floor. She hesitated in the wide doorway for a moment and then saw her friend Mary Sullivan, who was also a nurse on the surgical floor. Mary waved to indicate there was an empty seat at her table. Judy nodded and then joined the line at the counter and took a tray. When she had gotten her usual salad she carried it directly to the table for two where Mary was sitting.

"How did things go in O.R.?" Mary wanted to know.

Judy sighed. "It was cancer all right. But Dr. Holland was marvelous as usual. I think he got it all and Mr. Ames has a chance." Mary had also been one of the accountant's nurses and so knew him.

"I guess you were glad to scrub for Dr. Holland again," Mary said.

"It's an experience," Judy agreed, as she began on her salmon salad. She said nothing about the alarming slowness with which the operation began, feeling the veteran surgeon had more than made up for it later. But a small nagging worry still continued at the back of her mind.

"If I had your training, I'd ask for operating room duty full time," Mary Sullivan said.

Judy smiled at one of the interns as he passed on his way out. "I don't like it that much," she said. "But I do want to work under Dr. Holland whenever I can."

Mary's black eyes twinkled behind her glasses. "Not to mention the charming Miles Small!"

Judy shrugged. "He's not a bad surgeon."

"But you don't think he's a good one," Mary said with a faint smile.

"Don't put words in my mouth," Judy laughed. "I get in enough trouble doing that myself. What I meant is, he doesn't measure up to Dr. Holland's standards."

"You could hardly expect him to. Dr. Holland is the best we have. He's given his life to his career. He's an old man now."

"I know," Judy agreed as she stared down at her plate. She had been keenly conscious of this at the operating table this morning. For a short time she'd known real fear. Yet, in the end it had all gone well.

Mary sipped her coffee. "You're going to the dance with Dr. Small tonight, aren't you?"

"Yes. What about you?"

The girl let a look of disgust cross her

plain face. "I'm on the lunch committee. They knew no one would ask me to go, so out of the goodness of their hearts they invited me to attend and work. I'll probably wind up passing you sandwiches."

"At least you'll be there," she said. "I wonder if it will be as gala an affair as last year."

The benefit dance was held at the country club early in June every year. It was strictly a social event, attended primarily by the members of the various committees associated with the hospital as well as the board.

"Looks like plenty of action upstairs this afternoon," Mary said, changing the subject as she referred to the surgical floor. "We've got several new patients coming in and a couple being readied for surgery in the morning."

"How is Gallant Bess?" Judy asked with a wry expression and took a sip of her milk.

"Rampant!" Mary said. "I think she is jealous of Dr. Holland's picking you out to help him when his regular scrub nurse isn't available. Bess considers herself the most competent scrub nurse in the entire northeastern United States and maybe the whole continent."

"She's floor supervisor and takes every

opportunity of throwing her weight around," Judy complained. "I should think that would satisfy her. Especially since she really isn't up to the job."

She was talking about Mrs. Bess Raymond, the plump, middle-aged head nurse of the surgical floor during the day shift. She had returned to hospital work because of the shortage of nurses after long years as a housewife. They soon learned to avoid the overbearing woman as much as possible since she continually talked about her husband, who was a semi-invalid after two serious heart attacks. They were brought on, Mary had emphatically declared, by his wife's sharp tongue and her two teenage sons, who were destined to be outstanding college material and later leaders in the business community.

The henna-haired, overweight woman did more than brag — she dreamed aloud. All the nurses on the floor were disgusted with her, and several times she had made careless mistakes and blamed one of her underlings for it. On one of these occasions when Mrs. Raymond had made an error in a doctor's instructions concerning the dosage of a potent drug, Judy had refused to carry out her orders. Though this had created a scene, Judy was proved right. However, the head nurse, who was jealous of her in any case, apparently had held it against her, and now she always tried to make it as difficult as possible for Judy. Because the stout woman was continually referring to her own ability and courage in the face of desperate odds, the nurses on the floor had taken to laughing behind her back and tagging her Gallant Bess!

Mary shook her head. "Two or three times this morning she made one of her snide remarks about managing to get along without Dr. Holland's favorite."

"I like that!" Judy said indignantly, pushing her empty milk glass away. "Surely she doesn't think he should have picked her."

They took the elevator up to the fourth floor where the surgical cases were. As soon as they stepped out, they saw Head Nurse Raymond in serious discussion with Dr. Leon Grant, one of the younger surgeons, in the nurses' room. Mary gave Judy a knowing look and went down the corridor. She was about to go in the opposite direction when the head nurse looked out through the wide, open section in the wall of the nurses' room and saw her.

"Here is Nurse Scott," she said in her strident tones and with a look of smug satisfaction on her face. "I'll let her look after your case, Doctor."

Dr. Grant showed slight surprise at this and vaguely smiled his thanks to her. Then he came out through the door of the nurses' room to stand facing Judy. He was a serious-looking man with receding brownish hair that emphasized a forehead ordinarily high.

"I've just admitted a woman patient," he said, in the confidential manner he always used. "A Mrs. Frances Pomeroy, perhaps you have heard of her. She's a widow. Operates the big flower shop on Grand Street and has a giant hothouse on the road to Providence."

"I've passed the hothouse and seen her signs," Judy said, wondering what he was leading up to.

He cleared his throat. "She may turn out to be a difficult patient," he said. "I'm trying to get her a private nurse, but so far I've had no luck. She's in for observation. I suspect we'll have to remove the gall bladder. She's had several severe attacks."

"I see," Judy nodded. "If she's inclined to be difficult and can afford it she should certainly have a private nurse."

"I'm trying to arrange for one during the day if I can," Dr. Grant agreed. "In the

23

meanwhile I'll depend on you to do your best. Mrs. Raymond assures me you are equal to the most temperamental case."

"I wouldn't say that," she said, knowing full well that this was probably a neat little trap Head Nurse Raymond was setting for her. "Do you want me to go look in on your patient now?"

Dr. Grant glanced at his watch quickly. "Yes, do that," he said. "I'd come along with you but I'm due downstairs at this very minute." He turned to step into the elevator, then paused to add, "You'll find her in 423."

Judy was still mystified as she watched the elevator doors close and cut him off from her. He had certainly been in a great hurry to be on his way. She seriously doubted his instant need to appear in the lobby below. As she made her way down the wide corridor to room 423 she had the feeling she was due for a surprise and it might not be a pleasant one.

It wasn't! When she went into the private room bearing the number 423 she discovered an immense woman with a broad red face, scraggly blond hair that was obviously dyed, and small suspicious eyes. She glanced at Judy.

"Who are you?" she demanded. "My private nurse?"

24

"No," Judy said, managing a smile. "I'm Nurse Scott, one of the regular staff. Dr. Grant has asked me to keep a watch on you until you get a private duty nurse." She paused. "Are you comfortable?"

The big woman propped against the pillows snapped, "I am not! And I want my briefcase! Dr. Grant let one of your stupid nurses take it away."

Judy frowned. "Are you sure?" she asked. "It may be in the closet here." She came nearer the bed, and the big woman's breath reached her giving her a jolt! Mrs. Pomeroy might deal in flowers but she smelled of whiskey!

"It's not here!" the big woman raged. "I've looked. And there's something in it I want."

Judy saw it was useless to argue with her. "I'll check with the head nurse," she said. Happy for an excuse to get out of the room, she left and went up the corridor to the nurses' station. Head Nurse Raymond was standing there with a blissful expression.

Judy explained about Mrs. Pomeroy's briefcase. "There are some papers or something in it she wants," she said.

The head nurse looked too happy as she walked away and returned with the case. Holding it up, she took a liquor bottle from it. "Not this?" she said.

CHAPTER TWO

Judy stared at the half-empty bottle and was at once aware why Dr. Leon Grant had been so quick to beat a retreat. She also now knew why Head Nurse Raymond had seized the opportunity to put 423 in her hands. This was a grand opportunity for Gallant Bess to see that she suffered more than her share of headaches.

"Then she's an alcoholic," she said.

Head Nurse Raymond's face was smug. "We prefer not to refer to her by that term," she said, putting the bottle back in the brief-case. "You realize it is impossible for her to have this."

"You had better tell her," Judy said, "or let Dr. Grant do it."

"I'm afraid I'll have to depend on you," the head nurse said happily. As she spoke, the light in 423 flashed on the board. "She's asking for someone now," she added. "Better answer her and give her the good news at the same time."

Judy stood staring at the big woman defiantly for a moment, a pretty picture of exasperation with her cap pertly set on her auburn hair. At last she said, "I got off the elevator at exactly the right moment!" and turned and strode down the wide corridor.

Mrs. Pomeroy's small, mean eyes had a tinge of red in them as Judy entered this time. "You again?" she exclaimed.

"Yes," Judy replied firmly. "You put on the light. Is there something I can do for you?"

"There is! And you know it!" the big woman said angrily. "I'm still waiting for that briefcase."

Judy regarded her with dangerous calm for a moment, a warning gleam coming into the big brown eyes. "Mrs. Pomeroy," she said softly, "didn't Dr. Grant explain that this is a hospital? A place for very sick people."

"I'm sick," Mrs. Pomeroy declared. "And I need my briefcase."

Judy moved closer to the bed. "You may be sick, Mrs. Pomeroy, but you certainly do not need that briefcase. Probably having it around too much has helped put you where you are now."

The big woman considered this for an astonished moment and then she cried, "How dare you! You, you little nurse! Call Dr. Grant! I want to talk to him at once!"

"Dr. Grant has a great many patients who

need him badly," Judy went on in the same quiet tone, "and I happen to have other patients on this floor who must be taken care of. We do not have time to bottle-nurse you, Mrs. Pomeroy." And without waiting to hear the angry outburst this brought, she stalked out of the room.

Let Head Nurse Raymond answer when the light in 423 came on again, as it surely would, or she could send someone else. Judy intended to keep so busy she wouldn't be near the board when Mrs. Pomeroy sent out a distress signal next time.

There was an amputation case in 417. An elderly male diabetic who had just had his left leg removed above the knee. He had been making good progress but was very despondent about his loss. Mike Conroy had been a postman delivering mail on the same route for more man a decade and he knew this meant the end of that job for him. Judy had not seen him since the previous day.

"How are we this afternoon, Mr. Conroy?" she asked.

"I've got that pain again, Nurse," he complained.

"Did you speak about it to Dr. Small?" she asked, coming over to his bedside.

He nodded. "Yes. He calls it a phantom pain. I'd swear it was in my foot only I haven't any left foot now." He spoke with a bitter frustration evident in his tone.

She offered him a sympathetic look. "But that's how phantom pain acts," she said. "It is caused by an irritation to a cut nerve in the thigh."

The bald man groaned. "And do I have to go through the rest of my life suffering from pain in a foot that isn't even there?"

"Of course not," she said. "Didn't the doctor explain that this is only a temporary condition? In the very worst cases the pain vanishes within a month or two."

The man in the bed shook his head sadly. "Well, that's some comfort but I can't say whether my patience will last that long or not."

"You're helping to upset yourself," she said. "You worry too much."

"How long before I get out of here?"

"I think Dr. Small said in another week."

"I almost dread it," he said with a sigh. "What will I do? Sit around the house? Look out the window?"

She studied him earnestly. "You'd do much better if you tried learning to walk with your crutches. In another two months you'll be fitted for your new leg."

"New leg!" he said disgustedly. "I'll never learn to use it."

"Most people have no trouble. By the end of two or three weeks of practice with it you'll surprise yourself."

He frowned and repeated what she had heard so often before. "I was a postman. People on my route were like my friends. What am I going to do now?"

"Dr. Small mentioned that you had been promised an inside job."

"So I have, but I don't want it! I've lost my leg and everything else!"

"Not your life, Mr. Conroy," Judy reminded him.

Mike Conroy looked ashamed at himself. "I guess I have been talking too much," be admitted. "Sorry, Nurse." He gave her a wan smile. "Maybe if you'll give me a hand I'll try the crutches for a while. At least it will help get my mind off my problems!"

She smiled her willingness to assist him and helped him out of bed. He managed to get around the room several times awkwardly using the crutches and buoyed in courage by having her at his side. Then he settled down in the easy chair by the window.

He glanced out at the hospital lawn with its giant elms in full foliage and turning, smiled up at her. "I guess it will be pretty good to get out after all. It's not such a bad world."

She left feeling he was in a better frame of mind at least. She knew the amputation had been a great shock to him, but it astonished her that he was not more grateful for his life having been saved. He was well on the road to what would be a complete recovery. On the way up the corridor she met Mary Sullivan coming down with a medicine tray.

The dark girl wore a smile. "Big doings! Gallant Bess just had a showdown with Dr. Grant's boozy patient in 423."

"I expected that," she said. "Who won?"

"The odds are on Gallant Bess but the little lady in 423 is still belting her light. We have orders to ignore it until Dr. Grant gets here. She just put a call through to him downstairs."

"Happy days!" Judy said and they each went their separate ways.

The balance of the afternoon passed without any new excitement. Dr. Grant made a nervous appearance and managed somehow to quiet Mrs. Pomeroy and then left as hurriedly as he'd arrived. Judy was glad when the clock showed four and she was able to change and leave.

Judy drove straight home to Redmond Acres where she lived with Moira and her husband. She saw Paul's convertible in the driveway and so knew they were both there.

She parked her sedan beside the larger car and went inside.

Paul was standing in the living room giving casual attention to a news broadcast on the big television set at the far end of it. Hearing her, he turned and came out to the doorway of the luxuriously furnished room to smile at her.

"How are things at the hospital?" he asked. It was his usual question. He was a good-looking, rather tense young man with crew-cut dark hair and the air of a rising young executive.

"More business than we can handle," she said with a smile in return. "How about the store?" Paul was advertising manager of his father's department store.

He spread his hands. "We've had better days. I've got a special 'End of School' sale scheduled next week. If that doesn't draw, you can book me a room at your place."

"Let me know whether you want surgical or medical," she said.

"If the sale doesn't click you can book me in both," he laughed. "All set for the dance?"

"All I need to make it perfect is about a full night's good sleep," she said, dropping into a handy chair near the foot of the stairs. "I'm bushed and that drive through the

32

traffic finished me."

"You look great," he said. "Moira came into the store this afternoon and decided the dress she'd picked out wouldn't do. She wound up buying the most expensive gown in our specialty room and putting the poor kids there through an orgy of alterations."

Judy looked up at him with amusement. "The price you have to pay for having a beautiful wife."

He stuffed his hands in the pockets of his neat pin-striped blue suit and stood considering her glumly with feet spread slightly apart. "Sometimes I think I should have settled for a little less beauty."

She knew he really meant it. It worried her to know that Paul had not found complete happiness in his love for Moira — that he was still insecure and jealous of her.

She said, "You'll be proud when you walk into the club with her tonight and everyone looks your way."

"What are you going to wear tonight?" Paul asked.

"That old white thing of mine. You must have seen it a half-dozen times before."

Changing the subject, Judy said, "I worked in the operating room this morning. Dr. Holland did a magnificent removal of a lung tumor."

Paul's serious face showed interest. "That must be pretty demanding for a man of his age. He ought to be retiring any time now."

"I don't think Dr. Holland will ever retire," she said, but her face clouded slightly at the remembrance of his hesitation at the beginning of the operation, of that moment when she had a feeling he might turn the patient over to Miles Small.

"At that he's not liable to want to give up," her brother-in-law agreed. "When you come to think of it, medicine is his whole life. What else has he got?"

Judy frowned slightly. She knew Paul was right. She said, "I know very little about his personal life. He likes to paint and there are a couple of his landscapes in his office at the hospital. I think they are very good."

"Sunday painting would hardly make up for all the hours of excitement at the hospital," Paul said with slight scorn.

"I suppose not," she said. "I understand he lives alone in that big house on Lorne Row with only a housekeeper to look after him. I've never heard of his having any relatives. He's the typical old bachelor living chiefly for his career."

"You're wrong on at least one point," he said with a knowing smile. "Graham Holland isn't a bachelor — he's a widower."

She sat forward in the chair, really startled. "I've never heard him nor anyone else mention a wife," she said.

"It's a touchy subject in this town even after a quarter-century," he said. "But I've heard my mother and father discussing it. When Dr. Holland first came to Bedford he was married to a lovely Boston girl. They had a daughter three years old and a boy four. He was just the same as he is now, placing medicine above everything else, and I guess he gave very little time to his wife and children."

"I suppose he was building a practice," she said, "and getting started at the hospital. It couldn't have been easy for him."

Paul shrugged. "I expect you to be on his side but most of the people here weren't. As my folks tell it, they were sorry for the wife. One day the little girl contracted meningitis and died almost immediately. Holland's wife became bitter and in less than a year she left him. They were never divorced but she went out to the West Coast with the boy. They never came back and the story goes she died a few years ago without having ever seen him again."

"A tragic story."

"I guess you'd call it that," he said. "At any rate your Dr. Holland did have some romance in his life."

"I'm glad and I'm sorry," she said, getting up from the chair. "Sorry it didn't turn out better for him."

"Who is taking you to the dance tonight?"

She hesitated, thinking of some way to put off answering him directly, and deciding this wouldn't work out, she said, "Miles Small."

Paul frowned at once. "You're wasting your time with him."

Judy started up the stairs. "He's amusing."

Her brother-in-law's serious face showed distaste. "Is that what you call it? I'd say inane. And anyway, the only reason he wants to come around here is to see Moira!"

"Who is coming to see Moira?" It was Moira herself who put the question brightly to them both from the top of the stairs. She was wearing a blue dressing gown lightly tied at the waist. The blue set off her sensational brunette beauty. She had the exquisite features and slim grace of the magazine cover girl she had so often been.

Judy started up the stairs to meet her sister. "Dozens of people are coming," she said lightly to pass the awkward moment. "And dinner isn't ready or anything."

"I've got dinner in the oven and well

36

under way," Moira assured her and Judy didn't doubt this was true. For underneath Moira's facade of fragile beauty there existed a good cook and competent housewife. She asked, "Did Paul tell you about my new dress?"

"He mentioned it without any details. What's the color?"

"Green and it's Heavenly!" Moira declared. "As soon as I saw it, I knew I wouldn't be happy in that other one."

Judy laughed. "Well, just so long as you're happy. I have to take a quick shower before we have dinner, and I'd better rush or I'll never be ready on time."

Moira went on down to join Paul. From the bottom of the stairs she called up to Judy, "As soon as you've finished your shower come to the dining room. Dinner will be ready."

Judy promised she would and hurried down the hall to her own room on the south end of the house. It was a large, bright room in pink and white shades. She quickly undressed and stepped under the shower. Within a few minutes she felt refreshed and rested.

Afterward, as she slipped into her dressing gown and removed the plastic shower cap which she had used to protect her hair, she studied herself in the mirror and decided she didn't look as tired as she felt. She was eager to get downstairs and have dinner so she could resume dressing for the dance.

She knew Paul wasn't in the best of moods and now she was doubly sure it would be wiser to be ready when Miles arrived and meet him outside. It was odd that these two former friends now barely spoke to each other. Of course, most of the hard feelings had been caused by Paul's jealousy. To make it more unfortunate, Moira was not a tactful person and Miles seemed to derive actual pleasure from tormenting Paul and keeping the feud going.

Judy found it tiring and heartily wished it would come to an end one day. She'd told Miles that once, and he had been quick to tell her she could easily straighten out all the trouble by becoming his wife. So far she had been hesitant about the idea. She liked Miles, but did she love him?

When she went into the dining room Moira and Paul were already at the table. She helped herself to the lobster newburg Moira had set out on an electric warming plate, and hurried through her meal, anxious to get back to her room and begin dressing. She was soon through and excused herself to return upstairs.

Because she kept her curly hair cut short it presented no difficulty. Her white evening gown was like an old friend and an adaptable one. By using new accessories each time she wore it she was able to achieve a slightly different effect. Tonight she was wearing emerald green ear rings, necklace and bracelet to accent its dazzling whiteness. Her formal gowns included only this one and a similar one in black and while she knew they weren't exciting, they did an excellent job for the limited use she had for them. Most of the weekly dances at the Country Club on Saturday nights were informal and she had a number of casual dresses she wore on those occasions.

A shawl in emerald green silk completed her outfit for the occasion. Quickly picking up a matching evening bag, she rushed out of her room and downstairs.

She was relieved to find Paul and Moira were both still upstairs dressing. A glance at the clock on the hallway wall told her it was only ten to nine so she went into the living room and sat in an easy chair where she had a view of the street outside. She would be able to see Miles' car when he drove up and go right out to meet him.

Just then his car came to a smooth halt in

front of the house and she quickly got up and went to the door. She was already on the front steps by the time he reached the sidewalk. He looked handsome and debonair in his white dinner jacket and his big car, like everything else about him, had an air of casual elegance.

"Looking especially desirable," he said approvingly, "and exactly on time!" He shook his head. "You must have some dreadful secret vice to balance all this!"

She laughed. "I'm an impulsive onion eater. Especially at cocktail parties. I drive people from me in droves."

He held the car door open for her. "Paul and Moira haven't left yet?"

"You know Moira," she said. "That gal really takes time to get ready."

"I know," he laughed good-naturedly. "She's nearly always late. But when she finally shows up, isn't it worth it?"

He said it with such a tone of enthusiasm mixed with wonder that she gave him an alarmed glance. The expression of remembered pleasure on his handsome face made her think that a lot of Paul's jealousy of him and Moira might be warranted. For a troubled moment she wondered if they still might be seeing each other secretly.

CHAPTER THREE

Before she could make any comment, Miles spoke again, changing the subject. "I checked on our morning patient in the recovery room. He seems to be doing well."

"I'm glad," she said. "I hope there wasn't any spread of the cancer that we missed."

"Dr. Holland searched pretty thoroughly," he said. "I'd be willing to bet we caught it early enough." He paused. "I thought you seemed a little nervous at the table when we first began."

"I was," she said. "It's been quite a time since I've worked in O.R."

"You're good at it. You should join us permanently."

"I've talked about that before," Judy told him. "Somehow I prefer to divide my time. I think you people have a tendency to become pure technicians and forget that patients are people. At least, a lot of the supervising nurses I've met in surgery have struck me that way."

Miles looked faintly amused. "I'd be willing to argue that point, but we'll call a truce since we are on the way to a party." He paused briefly. "I may as well admit I was on edge when we began the operation this morning. Chiefly, because it seemed for a moment Dr. Holland had taken some sort of spell. I looked your way and saw that you'd noticed it."

"I was aware of it," she admitted, "and it did alarm me even though he came out of it quickly enough."

"It certainly wasn't anything to worry about," Miles said.

"I wonder," she observed with a sigh. "You must have noticed he's looked bad lately. We tend to think of him as someone who will go on forever. But that's not so. What happened this morning points this up clearly enough."

He glanced at her with surprise. "I think you're making too much of it. He only faltered a moment. He's probably over-tired. As you know he's been carrying a heavy schedule of operations lately."

"That's true," she agreed.

She stared out the side window with a small frown on her pretty face. It made her unhappy to think of the old man failing. In her short period in Bedford she had come to admire him more than any doctor she had known. She would feel a distinct personal loss if he should be forced to give up his

42

work. Yet she couldn't shut her eyes to the alarming change in him lately.

She turned to ask Miles, "How old is Dr. Holland?"

"In his late sixties," he said. They were on the main highway now and coming to the open shore country where the country club was located.

She said, "Surgeons age quickly. A lot of them aren't operating at his age."

"Yet, many of them are."

"Granted," she agreed. "But Dr. Holland has been carrying the extra executive burden of being head of the hospital. I think he should either give that up or stop operating."

"We need him as a surgeon," he said.

"Then he should turn over his executive duties to someone else."

Miles smiled at her. "You're living up to your reputation for outspokenness, Nurse Scott," he said in bantering fashion. "There might be a lot of others to agree with you. Holland doesn't socialize enough to please the board. It annoys my father. As an example, you can be sure he won't show up tonight."

"Dr. Holland never attends hospital benefits," she said. "I don't think that is so important. He has a right to conserve himself if his health isn't up to par. But I wonder if his management of the hospital isn't open to criticism?"

Miles showed concern. "Have you heard anything along that line?"

"There has been some talk."

"There's always talk!" he said with a touch of irritation. "Not much of it has any foundation. Whenever anyone has a grievance, real or imagined, he gives Dr. Holland the blame!"

"Don't condemn me too quickly," she said with a rueful smile. "I'm on your side and Dr. Holland's. I'm as loyal as you are to the old man. But some things do make me wonder."

They had come to the big asphalt parking lot of the club and already there were quite a few cars there. Miles brought the car to a halt and turned to her as he switched off the motor.

"You're hopeless," he said. "Once you've made up your mind you've made up your mind!"

"Because I believe I'm right," she said earnestly. "I know where he stands as a surgeon. At the top of the list. But what about his judgment as an executive? You must admit it's an entirely different field, and it's as an executive that I believe him to be weak."

"I watch him in that capacity every day," Miles said, "and I see no reason to question his fairness or qualifications as a business man."

Judy thought uncomfortably they shouldn't remain seated in the parked car too long talking or the gossips would snatch on to that as a subject of speculation, but she did want to hear the young surgeon out. Now that they had brought the subject of Dr. Holland into the open, she wanted to explore it thoroughly.

"You sound very sure," she said.

"I am," Miles said. "As an example, he recently approved the appointment to our staff of a young surgeon, a man whom I happen to know he doesn't care for personally. Yet, because it seemed best for the hospital, he went along with the appointment."

Judy was interested. "Who is the young man?"

"A new surgeon in town. Set up practice here last fall and he's been making a name for himself. He's been working over at St. Mary's but their facilities are limited and he felt he could do better for his patients at Bedford City. When he first applied for staff membership Dr. Holland was ready to turn him down."

"That doesn't sound like smart executive

thinking to me," she pointed out.

"There were sound reasons," Miles said. "We are heavy on surgical service and a newcomer could cause conflicts. Also, he seemed to have doubts about the young man's qualifications."

"But he did change his mind in the long run. So the reasons couldn't have been too valid."

"Dr. Holland agreed to accept him when we'd all taken it for granted it would be the opposite. Said he supposed no real harm would be done and that he didn't want to stand in the way of a younger man."

"Doesn't that suggest a weary, opinionated old man?" Judy wanted to know.

Miles smiled. "No. To me it suggests a very fair one."

"Yet, it seems you others on the board had to push him into the decision," she argued. "I'm not taken with that kind of leadership. I still say he should retire as hospital head. And you haven't told me the name of the new surgeon yet."

"John Randall," he said. "You should be meeting him soon at the hospital and I'll introduce you if he's here tonight. I understood he was coming with Dr. Morgan Staples and his wife. He's been seeing the Staples girl since he came to town."

Judy rolled her eyes in despair. "Not Betty Staples!"

Dr. Staples was the town's psychiatrist and was not regarded as a very competent practitioner in the field by most of the other medical men. It was said two outstanding examples of his failure were his utterly fatuous wife and his pretty but flirtatious and vacant-minded daughter Betty. They could have both received benefits from good psychiatric advice.

"The same Betty Staples," Miles grinned. "I don't say that's an indication of his taste since he's a bachelor and new to the city. Likely he was lonely and they took him in."

"Took him in is right," Judy said. "They've been looking for a husband for Betty for quite awhile now. We'd better go inside or people will think we're out here plotting something dire."

He seemed reluctant to get out of the car. "I'm enjoying myself here," he said. "I don't care much what they think."

"I do," she said firmly.

They walked across the parking lot, pausing to let a black limousine with one of the board members at the wheel pass. Once inside the club they found the reception committee already lined up at the door of the ballroom.

As they made their way in Miles said, "Now we run the gauntlet!" He spoke in a low voice that couldn't be heard by anyone else and she had a hard time suppressing a smile.

Both of Miles' parents were on the committee.

White-gloved Mrs. Small offered her a cordial smile and took her hand in a light grasp. "How pretty you look, dear," she said. "I hope you and Miles have a lovely evening."

"I'm certain we will," she said politely as she moved on to the ex-governor himself.

Brandon Small had a shrewd eye and the same elegance of manner as his son. "Save a dance for me," he said, making it seem a very wicked and important request.

She laughed when he punctuated his request with a wink. "You'll have to clear it through Miles," she warned him.

They finished the line and Miles, looking slightly harried, said, "There's music. Why shouldn't we begin dancing?" Suiting the action to the word, he swept her into his arms and led her out amid the couples already on the floor.

Newcomers kept arriving and by the time Miles and Judy had danced the medley of numbers the ballroom was nearly filled. The decorations were colorful and everyone seemed to be having an excellent time.

A party of the doctors and their wives arrived and Judy was amused to note Dr. Leon Grant among them. She wondered what new difficulties he might have with Mrs. Pomeroy. Then, as this group moved on, she saw Moira and Paul coming in. Moira was truly radiant in the green creation and Paul looked both sulky and proud.

They were lucky enough to find a table for two near the wall and they divided their time between it and dancing. The ex-governor made his usual neat, rather pompous speech and not long afterward came to claim his dance with Judy.

"Why don't you make Miles bring you to the house once in awhile?" Mr. Small asked as they danced. "We'd enjoy having you."

"We've both been so terribly busy," she told him. The truth of the matter was that Miles had pressed her to visit with his parents, but she had consistently refused as she didn't want to get tagged as Miles Small's girl friend. This would certainly follow in a town the size of Bedford. People would next be scanning the social columns for their engagement notice.

"I'll speak to him about it," Brandon

Small promised as they finished their dance. "We'll look forward to seeing you for dinner soon."

It was nice to know his parents liked her. The unhappy fact was she wasn't interested in Miles beyond his charm as a social partner, so it didn't really matter whether they approved or not. She supposed if she were truly serious about him the approval of his parents would have been welcome. Especially since they weren't the kind to bestow it lightly.

Midway through the dance that followed, Miles hesitated. "I see Dr. John Randall and Betty Staples over there. The old folks have left them alone a minute. Let's go over."

With his usual impulsiveness he at once guided her across to the long table where pretty, blonde Betty Staples sat in the company of someone whom Judy at first took to be an extremely surly young man. On second glance she decided this might be modified to serious. At any rate, he was staring at her with undisguised interest and she had the feeling he was bored with his lovely companion.

Miles exerted all his polished charm on Betty as he bent over her hand. "You look ravishing tonight, Betty, positively ravishing. I must have a dance with you." He turned to introduce her. "Of course, you know Judy?"

"Yes!" Betty smiled broadly, drawing the single word out until it was a sort of silly sentence ending on a high squealing note.

"I want Judy and Dr. Randall to meet," Miles went on suavely as he made the proper introductions. Then, without waiting, he led the slightly-dazed Betty off with him.

The large hazel eyes of the town's new surgeon were fixed on Judy as if she were some extremely new and interesting species. His appraisal was grave. Without a smile, he said, "Would you care to dance?"

"I think so," she said lightly, somewhat amused by his sober demeanor. He walked to the edge of the dance floor with her and took her in his arms as they joined the other couples. He had a rather square face that couldn't be called good-looking, yet, it had character and honesty. This was not a weak face and already lines of living had etched themselves in the tanned skin. He wasn't much taller than Judy but his body was muscled and his shoulders were wide. His dark brown hair had a slight curl that gave him a romantic air rather out of keeping with the rest of him.

He said, "So you're with the Bedford City Hospital?"

She smiled. "Yes. I hear you're going to join us."

"Yes. I'm about to be admitted to your exclusive circle," he said with a hint of bitterness.

"You'll like Dr. Holland," she promised.

"On the contrary," he said. "I don't care for him at all."

It was such a surprising and flatly stated comment she couldn't ignore it. At once, all her loyalty for the veteran surgeon surged up in her. She studied the young man dancing with her with a perplexed smile.

"But you can hardly know him? How can you form an opinion so quickly?"

"Part of my professional training, if you like," he said in his calm serious way. "Dr. Holland and I seemed to take an instant mutual dislike for each other. It happens that way occasionally. He has tried very hard to keep me off the Bedford City staff."

"I understand he gave way to your appointment of his own accord."

The hazel eyes showed a small gleam of interest, but the square face remained expressionless. "Is that so?" he inquired politely.

Judy didn't know what to make of him. She certainly wasn't impressed by his manner. She said, "Dr. Holland is a fine surgeon. I've scrubbed for him often."

"I didn't know you had operating room experience," Randall said. "Are you on the O.R. staff?"

"I just fill in once in awhile."

The music stopped and he looked around the room and then at her. "I'd like to talk a little longer with you," he said. "Is there somewhere we could go for a stroll? It should be very nice out tonight and it's hard to talk with Betty around, she's . . ." at this point he stopped, seeming unable to properly find words for Betty.

Judy smiled. "There's a patio. I'll show you the way. I could do with some fresh air myself."

The patio opened off the ballroom. There were already a half dozen couples standing at various points along its railing. There was a fine view of the ocean, a vision of silver splendor now under the magic of a full moon.

The conversation between her and the Dr. Randall now took on a general tone, and aside from the views he'd expressed about Dr. Holland, she found him agreeable and interesting. It didn't take her long to judge him by the opinions he expressed on various matters, and she decided that he was a remarkably smart young man who would certainly make his mark in his chosen field. More encouraging, he seemed to have the same dedication to medicine she had found in Dr. Holland.

She said, "What field of surgery are you specializing in?"

"General surgery," he said, "especially the abdomen. It's a vital area and yet a lot of doctors somehow pass it up for some other specialty."

"It sounds practical," she said.

"I always try to be." He was still very solemn and she began to wonder if he knew how to smile.

"You'll forgive me," she said. "But you seem a very serious sort of person."

He shrugged, his hazel eyes still fixed on her. "I laugh when I see something that amuses me but I admit that doesn't happen too often."

"You need to develop your sense of humor," she advised. "All people in medicine should. We're faced with so much that is tragic it could be overwhelming without the saving grace of humor."

"I agree with you in principle," he said politely. "I'll try to put your suggestion into practice more often."

Judy hadn't heard this last for her attention had been drawn to the French doors opening onto the patio. Miles had just emerged impatiently, dragging a confused Betty Staples after him. He was looking around in what was obviously a feverish attempt to locate them.

Judy touched her companion's arm and said, "See Miles!" She was trying hard not to laugh. "It seems Betty has driven him to distraction!"

"I wouldn't wonder," Dr. Randall agreed. Glancing at Judy, he smiled for the first time. "I suppose I'd better rescue him. I hope we meet soon again."

As soon as they were alone again Miles looked at Judy indignantly and said, "That was a nice trick you played on me!"

She smiled at him with mock innocence. "But you said you wanted me to meet Dr. Randall."

"I didn't expect you'd spend the rest of the evening with him," he said. "To make it worse, you know what I think about Betty!"

"I'm sorry," she said. "But he wanted to talk and he seemed to know we wouldn't have a chance if we went back where Betty was."

Miles shook his head. "The only girl I know who carries on a conversation with one syllable words and makes them sound like sentences."

"Dr. Randall is really a nice young man," she said. "Even if he doesn't like our Dr. Holland."

Miles arched an eyebrow. "You got around to that?"

She nodded. "We hit most of the important points. I think he'll change his mind about Dr. Holland after he comes to work at the hospital."

"That might be where you are mistaken," he pointed out.

"I hope not," she said sincerely.

Miles smiled at her. "Randall better watch out. I know whose side you're on!" He took her by the arm and they made their way to the French doors and inside.

The dancing had ended for a time and the lights in the ballroom were turned up brightly as refreshments were passed around. Almost the first one to come up to Judy and Miles was Mary Sullivan carrying a huge tray of sandwiches.

"My part of the gay evening," she said, a wry smile on her face. She hadn't removed her heavy-rimmed glasses, but she had fixed her hair attractively. Also, she wore a yellow dress that suited her dark complexion and she looked very nice.

Judy whispered to her, "You look wonderful!"

Mary showed pleasure at the compliment. "I feel a lot more comfortable in my uniform," she said. Then she moved on to another couple.

After the refreshments there was more dancing. It was well past midnight when Miles drove Judy home. He was in a talkative mood and she had to keep reminding him they were both due to be at the hospital early.

"I can solve that for you," he smiled across at her in the shadowed front seat of the car.

"Really? You'll put in a good word for me with Gallant Bess, I suppose."

"Nothing like that," he said. "Marry me and I'll allow you to sleep as late as you like every morning."

It was Judy's turn to smile. "It's a tempting offer," she said, "I'll give it plenty of thought."

"It's not an offer," he assured her, "it's at least my fourth proposal and each time you've promised to think it over. How much thinking can a girl do?"

"Never too much in this case," she said.

He shook his head. "Action is the only answer!" He proceeded to demonstrate this by taking her in his arms for a long kiss. When he finally released her, he held up a hand in warning, "I know what you're about to tell me," he said, "and don't do it. I'll let you go. You have to be at work at seven in the morning!"

He got out of the car and saw her to the door, saying goodnight again in his mocking light-hearted manner. She watched him drive away and then went inside. Paul and Moira were already home and had gone upstairs to bed. Judy went up to her own room as quietly as she could and then quickly changed into her nightgown.

It had been an exciting evening, and tired as she was, sleep did not come at once. She thought of all that Miles had said and recalled his goodnight kiss with a special tenderness. But it was something else that stood out in her memory. The moment when the sober Dr. John Randall had turned to her and smiled.

CHAPTER FOUR

Gallant Bess regarded Judy with a surly expression when she entered the nurses' station the next morning. "I suppose you had a wonderful time," the head nurse said with a note of sarcasm. "You look like skimmed milk!"

"I didn't get much rest," Judy said frankly, "but it was fun. You should have gone." She said this to get the big woman's reaction more than anything else since she knew the head nurse wouldn't have fitted in at the party.

Mrs. Raymond glared at her. "As a wife and mother I have more important things to do."

"There were a lot of wives and mothers there," Judy said innocently.

The big woman tossed her head. "I've been to more dances than you're ever likely to see. When you're my age, you won't be so anxious to jump around half the night." As she finished speaking, the light in 423 blinked on violently and the head nurse observed it with some satisfaction.

"Seems you're in luck," she said malevolently. "Mrs. Pomeroy is your first call."

Judy looked grim. "If she makes too much fuss, I just might give her the briefcase with that bottle after all." She marched off to 423 leaving a thoroughly startled Gallant Bess behind her.

When she went into the private room occupied by Mrs. Pomeroy, the drapes were still drawn and the big woman was stretched out groaning. Judy first opened the drapes and then went over to the bedside to take a good look at the patient.

"Can I do something for you?" she asked politely.

The small beady eyes in the broad red face gazed up in distress. "I'm dying," the big woman announced with a loud groan.

Judy had a pretty fair idea of what was causing all the suffering on Mrs. Pomeroy's part but she couldn't help feeling a little sorry for her. It seemed Dr. Grant might have warned her against this long dry spell before entering her in the hospital. But if he had done that, perhaps she would not have come, and she was supposed to have a severe gall bladder condition.

Knowing better, she said, "Is there anything I can get you?"

The small eyes closed. "My briefcase," the red-faced woman said weakly from her pillow.

"I'm afraid that's impossible," Judy told her. "But surely I can help you some other way. Have you had breakfast?"

"Can't eat," Mrs. Pomeroy protested, her eyes still shut. One of her large hands grasped the bed covering in the area over the upper right part of her abdomen. "Got this awful pain!"

At once the situation became different in Judy's eyes. She knew the big woman had come in for X-rays and examination yesterday for a gall bladder condition, and now it looked as if she'd been stricken by a serious attack. If so, it could be a dangerous situation and Dr. Grant should be alerted at once.

"Have you told anyone else?" she asked.

"No one will listen," the big woman gasped, "think I'm a crazy drunk!"

"I'm sure they don't think that," Judy said, more from politeness than truth, "and we do want to help you. When did this pain start?"

"In the night!" Mrs. Pomeroy twisted and groaned again.

Judy now gave more attention to the woman's face and saw that it had taken on a yellowish tinge. This confirmed her fears and made her suspect Mrs. Pomeroy had likely become jaundiced. The most logical explanation of this was that a stone had lodged in the common bile duct at the exit into the intestine. The entire flow of bile duct would be obstructed and this condition demanded urgent surgery.

She said, "Have you had attacks like this before? As much pain?"

"I've had spells but never so bad." Her eyes opened and she gazed up at Judy forlornly. "This time I've really got a knife twisting around in there!" She moaned again.

Judy waited to make a temperature check of the patient and found it was very high. Then she tried to make her more comfortable before she hurried out and went up the corridor to present the situation to Head Nurse Raymond.

"Who saw Mrs. Pomeroy this morning?" she asked.

The head nurse frowned. "I looked in on her a moment myself. She was having a time. Putting on a grand show, hoping I'd take pity and give her a drink of that whiskey, I suppose."

"There's more to it than that. I think she has an acute gall bladder attack. You'd better get in touch with Dr. Grant at once."

Mrs. Raymond looked suspicious. "Are you certain?"

"I am, and I don't think there is any time

to lose. Tell him the patient shows jaundice and has terrible spasms of pain."

Gallant Bess looked annoyed as she sat down to the phone. "I don't know where we can reach him at this time."

"Surely his telephone answering service can tell you that," Judy insisted, annoyed at the slowness with which the head nurse was approaching the problem. Remembering, she added, "Is Dr. Holland in his office? Wasn't he going to do the operation with Dr. Grant assisting?"

"Dr. Grant said something like that," Mrs. Raymond frowned, obviously thinking it over slowly.

"Then you should contact Dr. Holland first," Judy advised. "Someone should check that woman right away."

It finally got through to the head nurse. She picked up the telephone and asked to speak with Dr. Holland. Glancing over her shoulder at Judy, she scowled and said, "I hope this is no false alarm!" Then, as Dr. Holland came on at the other end of the line, she spoke sweetly in her most professional manner. "I am sorry to bother you, Doctor, but we have a patient of Dr. Grant's here who seems to be having trouble. I thought you should see her. It's a Mrs. Pomeroy." There was a short pause while

63

she listened to his reply. Then she said, "Thank you, Doctor," and hung up. She turned to Judy. "He's coming up at once. He knows all about her. Saw her plates this morning and says she has a serious condition."

"It's worse now," Judy said.

"I'll try to get Dr. Grant," Mrs. Raymond said, picking up the phone again.

Judy went out to the corridor and Mary Sullivan appeared from the supply room. "You look as if you didn't get any sleep at all," Mary said.

"I didn't get much," Judy admitted with a wan smile, "and to start off the day we have Mrs. Pomeroy with a bad gall bladder attack."

"That's the lush in 423," Mary said callously. "Are you sure she knows what's wrong with her? She was pretty mixed up yesterday."

"I don't think there's any doubt now," Judy said. "She's ill."

At that moment the elevator door opened and Dr. Graham Holland stepped out. The veteran doctor had a worried expression on his lined face and seeing Judy, he asked, "What about Mrs. Pomeroy?"

"I've just come from her, Doctor," she said. Glancing in the window of the nurses'

64

station she saw that the head nurse was still on the phone. "Mrs. Raymond is trying to get Dr. Grant," Judy went on. "I'll take you down to the patient. She is in 423."

Actually, the old man strode down the corridor ahead of her at a pace she found difficult to keep up with. He made his way to Mrs. Pomeroy's bedside and one look at her apparently told him all he needed to know.

He leaned over the bed to speak reassuringly to Mrs. Pomeroy. "Don't you worry about a thing," he told her. "We'll have you out of this pain in no time." The woman on the bed answered with a groan.

Dr. Holland accompanied Judy back to the nurses' station, giving her instructions regarding medication for the stricken woman. Mrs. Raymond was waiting for them anxiously.

"I've reached Dr. Grant," she said. "He will be here shortly. Is she any better, Doctor?"

The stern bulldog face showed worry. "I had planned to operate later in the week. It can't be put off now. I'll have to clear an operating room and get her downstairs as quickly as possible." He glanced at Judy absently. "It looks as if I'll have to call on you to scrub again, Miss Scott."

Head Nurse Raymond gave her an exasperated look. "I'll put a call in for one of the student nurses to fill in until you get back," she said. There was no question that she resented Judy going to the O.R. again.

The next half-hour passed at a frantic rate with Judy turning over the care of Mrs. Pomeroy to Mary Sullivan, Dr. Grant arriving breathless and still suspicious that his patient might be pretending, although he soon discovered this was not the case, and Judy hurrying to the operating room to prepare for the emergency surgery.

This morning they would use the smaller operating room which Dr. Holland had managed to clear for the period necessary by having one of the other surgeons postpone a scheduled appendectomy until the late afternoon.

Jean Stephens, who would be circulating nurse, was already in the O.R. preparing for the arrival of the surgeons and Mrs. Pomeroy. It was a modern room that had recently been updated and its gleaming tile and metal fairly shrieked efficiency and sterility.

The operating table under the latest design overhead light was slightly different from the one in the larger O.R., being more compact. The anesthesia machine at its head was identical with the one in the other room as were the Mayo stands, the main instrument table and the suction machines.

Jean Stephens paused at the instrument table to turn and say, "A rush one this time!"

Judy nodded. "Dr. Holland felt he couldn't delay."

Minutes later Mrs. Pomeroy was wheeled in, her large form motionless under a covering sheet, already in deep sleep from Pentothal Sodium. Then Dr. Granger, the middle-aged and slightly harried anesthetist, arrived.

He sighed as he came up to the operating table. "What a morning!" he said to Judy. "Half the regular schedule has been changed. I guess Dr. Holland wants an intercostal block anesthesia on this one."

Before she could make any reply Dr. Holland pushed his way in through the swinging door of the anteroom with his scrubbed hands held out in front of him.

"Dr. Grant will be right here," he told Judy as she opened his sterile gown and helped him into it. She continued helping him get ready as she powdered his hands and slipped on the rubber gloves. Then Dr. Grant arrived and she gave her attention to him.

The two doctors checked Mrs. Pomeroy's X-ray plates briefly again and then they were ready to begin the operation. After Mrs. Pomeroy had been thoroughly prepared and the field of surgery scrubbed and painted, Dr. Holland touched the foot pedal of the table to raise it a little. At the same time, Judy had moved the instrument stand up and swung the tray to a ready position.

"All right, Miss Scott," Dr. Holland said briskly and she handed him the scalpel.

As the operation proceeded, Judy saw that Dr. Holland was his usual efficient self. There was none of the early hesitation she had noted during the surgery the previous morning. He made brief comments to Dr. Grant as they worked. She found Dr. Grant's technique clumsy compared to Miles' and mentally classified him with the group referred to by O.R. nurses among themselves as the "butchers." He was careless with the knife and once Dr. Holland openly reprimanded him. After that, Dr. Grant was more cautious but Judy could see that he wasn't carrying his fair share of the operating load.

She glanced at the clock and saw that they had been there three-quarters of an hour. The normal time for this type of surgery was an hour, although Dr. Holland had sometimes successfully completed a gall bladder removal in half that time.

But not today! She knew by his comments they had run into complications. The clock passed the hour mark and then they were twenty minutes over the usual time.

"Two clamps!" The command came from Dr. Holland as a climax to a series that had kept her almost continuously busy. There was something strained in his tone as he made his request that caused her to give him a searching glance.

At once she saw the beads of perspiration trickling down his temples. "Miss Stephens, towel for the doctor," she said sharply. The circulating nurse at once stepped forward and deftly swabbed his temples.

The veteran surgeon was bent over the patient under the blinding light and hesitating now. He shook his head as if trying to clear it. Judy watched with growing alarm and a quick glance Dr. Grant's way revealed he was also aware of what was happening and there was a frightened gleam in his eyes.

"Something wrong, Doctor?" he asked solicitously.

The old man blinked his eyes and then the expert hands went to work again. "We've nothing to worry about now," he said, ignoring that the question had been about his own condition and referring to the patient.

From then on everything did proceed in a normal fashion. The clock showed the patient had been on the table an hour and forty minutes before she was wheeled out to the recovery room. Judy realized this wasn't too unusual since Dr. Holland had been faced with a complicated condition. But she knew that something had happened again to make her fear for the surgeon's state of health. He had obviously suffered some sort of dizzy spell midway through the operation and it had been more severe than the haziness of the previous day.

His eyes met hers as he took off his mask. His face was pale and he had a gaunt look she had never seen in him before. "Something bothered my eye a while back," he said. "A piece of dirt blew into it on my way to the hospital this morning. I thought I had it out, but it came back to bother me."

Judy was concerned, especially since she was almost certain he was concocting the story to cover up whatever had happened to him. She said, "Does it feel all right now?"

He nodded. "Surprisingly, it seems to have gone again. A cinder, I think. If it bothers me again I'll have someone check it for me." He turned to Dr. Grant, who stood by silently, looking somewhat shaken. "We'll soon have Mrs. Pomeroy on her feet again and able to enjoy her half-bottle of whiskey a day," he said jokingly.

"That's all she'll ask, Doctor," Dr. Grant said.

She knew the older surgeon had made his explanation to her mainly for Dr. Grant's benefit. This way there would be no awkward questions asked. But judging by the nervous younger man's reaction she doubted if he was any more satisfied by what Dr. Holland had said than she had been. A cinder in his eye! She doubted it very much.

By the time she finished cleaning up the O.R. it was noon and she went directly to the cafeteria. She had crossed the lobby and was on her way down the corridor leading to the cafeteria's wide entrance when she heard footsteps quickly coming up behind her. A moment later a hand touched her arm lightly and she turned to look up at Miles' smiling face.

He walked beside her. "Would you consider sharing your lunch hour with a struggling member of the medical profession or would you prefer a gossip session with some of your nursing associates?"

Judy gave him a rueful smile. "Something

tells me I'll have no choice."

"And, as usual, you're right," he said. "I have decided you shall be my luncheon guest."

She hesitated in the doorway with him to survey the crowded room with an amused expression. "And what an exclusive place you've chosen."

The tall blond man sighed. "Gallantry doesn't pay with you," he said. "Grab a tray and get in line."

Judy moved ahead and they picked up trays. Within a few minutes they had made their selections from the long counter of food on display. Then Miles led her through the maze of filled tables to a corner where there was an empty one. On the way she saw Mary Sullivan sitting alone at a table for two and, in all likelihood, waiting for her. The dark girl gave her a questioning look and Judy nodded to Miles striding ahead and shrugged.

When she and Miles were seated, he looked at her with a new expression, all his bantering manner vanished. "I wanted to ask you a few questions," he said. "I hear you were called on to scrub for Holland again this morning."

She had an idea what was coming and debated what she should say. "Yes. I just came from the O.R. now," she told him.

Miles carefully cut into his open steak sandwich. "So I heard. You were in there almost two hours weren't you?"

She looked up from her salad to smile. "Mrs. Pomeroy is a difficult patient whether she's awake or under anesthesia."

"I'll bet," he said. "Dr. Grant didn't seem to think it was all her fault you were in there so long, though."

"No?"

"No," he said, pausing to look directly at her. "He seemed to think Graham Holland had some sort of dizzy spell."

"He'd have plenty of time to notice," Judy said, with a hint of annoyance. "He wasn't doing much to help."

Miles nodded. "I know about Dr. Grant's limitations in surgery. What I don't know and would like to find out is, what happened to Dr. Holland?"

Judy thought rapidly. Her natural desire to cover up for the hospital chief was balanced by her knowledge that she might only harm him in the end by doing so. With a small sigh, she said, "It wasn't much. Something like yesterday only a little more noticeable and it happened later in the operation."

The young man opposite her warned,

"Keep your voice down. You don't know who might come by and draw some wrong conclusions."

She leaned across the table a little and in a low voice went on, "It seemed as if his vision was blurred for a moment. He hesitated and just when I was sure he might collapse, he seemed to recover from whatever it was and went on as if it had never happened."

"Grant said he looked awful afterward."

"That is true," she agreed. "I noticed it myself. And he offered an explanation about something in his eye bothering him."

"Which you don't believe?"

"I'm afraid not."

Miles sat back with a worried expression. "Yesterday could have been an exception. But when something like this happens twice in a row you can be sure it means trouble."

"Why don't you talk to Dr. Holland about it frankly?" she suggested.

He shook his head. "That wouldn't work. He'd only deny everything. You know what he's like."

"Perhaps, if you ignore it, the trouble will pass and he'll be all right."

"Or maybe one of these mornings he'll collapse at the operating table and leave someone like Grant to finish a complicated operation. I'll tell you it gave him a scare.

He was still trembling when he came to me with the story a few minutes ago."

"He didn't lose any time," Judy said with a touch of scorn.

"The man was frightened," Miles said seriously. "He knows he'd likely have botched that woman up if he'd had to finish on his own. You won't catch him venturing into the O.R. with the old man again if he can help it."

Judy stared glumly at her empty plate. "I suppose he'll spread the story all over the hospital."

"No. Grant knows when to keep his mouth shut. He told me but he'll let it stop at that. I'm wondering about the others who were in there. I can depend on you, and the students assisting wouldn't even notice. But what about the circulating nurse?"

"Jean Stephens," she said. "I'll speak to her and ask her not to say anything. I don't think she would anyway. She worships Dr. Holland."

He nodded. "Good. That leaves only Dr. Granger."

For a moment she had forgotten about the anesthetist. The irritable little man had a way of coming and going without attracting much attention. She said, "I don't know him very well."

"I do," Miles said grimly. "He's the very worst sort of male gossip. If he doesn't spread the good news around, I'll be surprised."

"Can't you ask him not to?"

"I could," he said. "But I know it wouldn't do any good. He'd say yes and go on talking just the same. The best thing in his case is not to mention it at all and hope he missed it."

"Maybe he did," she said doubtfully. "Meanwhile, what are you going to do?"

"I haven't decided," he said. "I may get desperate enough to try your idea and face him directly with it. First I'll talk it over with my father. He's a diplomat and a member of the hospital board. And he and Dr. Holland are old friends."

Judy's eyes were solemn. "I feel we do have a responsibility in this."

"I realize that," he said. "If he'd just take things a little easier."

"Give up as head of the hospital for a start," Judy said. "You should be able to persuade him after what has happened."

"You mean blackmail him into resigning?"

She blushed. "Blackmail is a nasty word."

"What you are suggesting is the same thing."

"No. I'm trying to think of a solution that will be right for him and the hospital, and most important, a solution that will protect the patients in our care."

The young surgeon's face was grim. "At least you're saying it plainly."

She said, "It's time for plain words. I'm sorry. I know it won't be easy for you."

He toyed with his empty coffee cup. "Did you enjoy the dance?"

"Very much."

"What do you think of John Randall?"

She shrugged. "Dr. Randall seems a very conscientious person. He's not easy to type. I'd say he lacks a sense of humor."

"Perhaps," Miles said. "Still, you may not know him well enough to judge properly."

"Could be," she said. "I'd expect him to be a perfectionist."

"All the reports on him have been excellent," he said. "And that includes the opinions of the nursing staff at St. Mary's. He seems to have a definite appeal to all you ladies."

Judy got up from the table. "It's time I stopped enjoying your company and went back to work," she said.

He walked toward the door with her. The cafeteria was not as busy now with many of the tables empty. She saw that Mary

Sullivan was among those who had already left. Miles got off the elevator on the mezzanine floor and Judy went on up to surgical.

Head Nurse Raymond had returned from lunch and was waiting to greet her. "So you're finally back," was her sour welcome. "We need you. It's been a madhouse here. And we've got patients coming in. That new man Dr. Randall is bringing his first patient in today."

Judy accepted the news with interest. It struck her as a wry twist of fate that Dr. Holland's angry young opponent should be beginning at the hospital on the very day the old man had shown definite signs of failing health. She hoped that with Randall's acceptance by the board, the hostility between the two men would be ended but knowing the aggressive characters of both of them, she was by no means sure.

CHAPTER FIVE

Not long after Judy went on duty, Calvin Ames was brought back from the recovery room. She supervised putting him in his own room and helped set up the array of stands and other paraphernalia that he would require for intravenous feeding and extra care during the first few days after his operation. He was very pale and she doubted that he recognized her as she did her best to make him comfortable.

Later, Miles came by to visit him and seemed very satisfied with his progress. "He's doing as well as we can expect," he told Judy. "He should have a private nurse for a day or so but the family hasn't mentioned it, so I guess you'll just have to give him all the attention you can."

"It's doubtful if they could get one anyway," she said. "There was a waiting list downstairs this morning. I think we can manage."

Head Nurse Raymond, who had overheard the conversation, registered an expression of displeasure. "Speak for yourself, Miss Scott," she said. "I don't promise anything. We're short on staff as it is."

Miles gave Judy a sly look. "Well, I'll just leave it in the hands of you capable ladies," he said, and beat a fast retreat to the elevator.

When she entered 417 she found Mike Conroy on his crutches and standing by the window. The man with the amputated leg turned around as he heard her come in and she was delighted to see that he wore a shy smile.

"Guess I surprised you," he said, swinging carefully around to face her. "Miss Sullivan helped me up on these and I've been working my way around the room for nearly half an hour."

"Being up and around will do you a lot of good," she said.

"I feel better today," he was ready to admit. "No more pain in that phantom toe. I suppose it'll come back again though."

"It may not," she said, "although it's likely that it will. Each recurrence of pain should be less intense. If it doesn't turn out that way, the doctor can correct it with minor surgery."

"I'm not eager to get on that operating table again," the former postman said. He looked down at his empty pants leg with a frown. "And I wish they hadn't taken my leg off above the knee. It's going to make it harder for me to wear an artificial leg."

Judy's eyebrows raked. "Who told you that?"

"A couple of the boys from the post office were in here yesterday and they thought it was a shame I didn't have my knee left. Said it helped a lot."

She said, "Well, they were wrong!"

"They were?" He showed surprise.

"Yes, and you can tell them next time they come, doctors never amputate any more tissue than they have to. They have to be sure there is good circulation at the point of amputation and that is why a site above the knee was chosen. And an artificial leg can often function better if the amputation is made above rather than below the knee."

Mike Conroy's face brightened. "Is that right?"

"It's generally true," she said with a smile. "So don't let uninformed people fill you full of nonsense tales. You tell them the facts."

"I'll be glad to, now that I know them myself."

Judy sighed. "It seems to me booklets telling something about the facts of amputations should always be given to patients undergoing one. It would save so much needless worry."

"I agree," he said.

"Of course, you'll learn all this later when you're being trained to use your new leg. But I think all the facts should be given early. And it's a fact a good artificial appliance is much more useful than an ailing or deformed limb."

She left the former postman in a happier frame of mind and headed back to the nurses' station where Mrs. Raymond announced, "That patient of Dr. Randall's has come in. She's in 439. You'd better go down and see that she is properly entered."

The patient in 439 was a frail, nervous little woman named Gertrude Miller. In taking down information Judy learned that she was divorced and had been employed as a school teacher for more than ten years. She had been ill on and off for the last two years and Dr. Randall had brought her into the hospital to have an ileostomy performed.

Judy found Mrs. Miller to be a typical victim of chronic ulcerative colitis, a serious inflammation of the large intestine. Most of the patients she had known with this trouble had, like Gertrude Miller, been in their thirties and of a highly neurotic and sensitive type. The new drugs such as penicillin, streptomycin and Terramycin occasionally cured the condition temporarily, but there was generally recurrence. It was such a recurrence that had brought the unhappy Mrs. Miller to the hospital. For the twenty-five per cent of those people dangerously ill with the disease, as she was, the only hope was surgery.

It was a difficult operation and up until now Dr. Holland was the only one who had had such patients at the Bedford City Hospital. A loop of the small intestine was brought out on the abdominal wall and opened. Thus intestinal contents drained out before reaching the diseased large bowel and this tended to allow the inflamed and ulcerated area to heal. In ten per cent of the cases the healing was so complete it was later possible to re-establish continuity and close the ileostomy. In most instances, however, the ulcers would not heal permanently and the artificial opening had to remain in the abdominal wall. Happily, it was possible for those having the operation to live completely normal lives afterward. It took the usual period of several weeks to adapt to the use of an airtight bag over the opening to seal off leaking and odors. Once this was accomplished the condition usually presented no problems.

After Judy had taken down all the information and made the usual checks of the patient, she said, "Dr. Randall will likely be along to see you soon."

"He promised he would," Mrs. Miller said with an uneasy look on her plain face. "I feel as though all this is going to leave me a cripple."

"Of course it won't," Judy said. "You'll be in much better health after the operation than you've ever been before."

She nodded. "That's what the doctor said. I'd like to believe it."

"You can."

Mrs. Miller eyed her anxiously. "How long do you think I will have to stay in the hospital?"

Judy considered. "I don't think it should be more than three weeks."

"Such a long time!" Mrs. Miller wailed.

She smiled. "It will pass quickly enough. And you won't want to plan doing much for a month or two afterward."

"School holidays are coming up," the thin woman said with a sigh of relief. "So that gives me a good two months, and I don't have to take any summer studies this year."

"You've chosen the ideal time," Judy said. "Try not to worry. It'll help you get better more quickly."

Mrs. Miller smiled apologetically. "Everyone says I'm a chronic worrier. I think some of us can't help it." She paused. "I won't need private nurses, will I?"

"You'll be in the recovery room for the most critical period," she said, knowing the woman probably could not afford private duty nurses although in most cases it was better to have them for such a serious operation. Well, they'd just have to give her extra care as they were doing with Calvin Ames now. No doubt Gallant Bess would huff and complain, but Judy knew that she and Mary Sullivan would have to do all the actual work.

For the balance of the afternoon Judy was kept busy with routine calls. She was bringing a tray of medicine from the drug room when the elevator door opened to reveal Dr. Randall.

He looked even more gravely sedate in a dark gray flannel suit, white shirt and crimson tie with a neat silver clasp than he had at the dance. He wore no hat and his curly brown hair had a slightly disheveled appearance. He carried his medical bag and when he saw her, his tanned, prematurely lined, face lit up.

"Miss Scott," he said. "Your uniform suits you. You should have worn one to the dance."

85

Still holding the tray, she paused to smile at him. "Didn't you approve of my gown?"

"It was perfect," he said. "But this outfit is you! Fits your personality perfectly."

"Thank you," she said, "your patient has arrived and is in 439. And you'll want to meet Mrs. Raymond, our head nurse."

She remained to make the proper introductions and then went on to make a final round with the various medications before leaving. When she had completed this task, it left her with only five minutes before the day shift was at an end.

Dr. Randall was standing by the nurses' station when she returned with her empty tray. His serious eyes studied her approvingly. "This is a well-run floor," he said. "I think I'm going to like it here."

"You have a serious operation to begin with," she said.

"I've done several ileostomies," he said, "and had good results with all of them."

She studied him with fresh interest. "You're lucky to have that experience. None of the doctors here seem anxious to touch them aside from Dr. Holland. He has always taken over patients requiring that type of surgery. All the other members of the staff prefer to refer such cases to him."

Something like a look of stubbornness

came into the young man's square face. "I won't have to do that," he said. "I know you often scrub for some of the surgeons here. I'd like to have you work with me when I operate on Wednesday."

She hesitated, "There are excellent girls on the regular staff. I only fill in for Dr. Holland once in awhile."

He offered her one of his rare smiles, revealing even white teeth. "I'd simply like to have you on my team for luck."

Judy gave a small shrug. "I would enjoy it, but you'll have to clear me with Mrs. Raymond first."

"I'll mention that before I go," he promised.

Judy hurried on her way to change, not wanting to be around when he spoke to the head nurse about her assisting him in the O.R. It would be a sure signal for another of her rages and she wanted to keep out of sight until the storm had passed. By tomorrow Gallant Bess would have forgotten.

It was another warm, sunny afternoon. When she finally reached the imposing house in Redmond Acres and parked her car, she found Moira, clad in brief halter and skimpy shorts of brilliant blue, sitting in a lawn chair out back reading the evening paper and enjoying the sunshine. When

Judy came around to take an empty chair near her, she removed her dark glasses and smiled.

"Isn't it gorgeous out here?" she asked.

"Better than a hospital corridor," Judy agreed with a sigh. "I've been pounding up and down one all day!"

Moira raised a shapely hand in a disgusted gesture. "Well, of course, you're such an idiot!" she said. "It isn't as if you had to go on working that way. You know Miles Small is dying to marry you. You could have a house up on the heights with a swimming pool and everything."

Judy studied her with tolerant amusement. "You know sometimes I think I shouldn't go on living here. You may be my older sister, but you're certainly a corrupting influence."

Moira showed pert shock. "What a thing to say!"

"Look at you!" Judy waved a hand wearily. "Reclining out here in all your natural glory. Skin tanned to a delicious shade, wearing the briefest and most expensive of sun outfits and having poor Paul as your willing slave." She glanced around. "Shouldn't your willing slave be home by now?"

"He's having that big sale at the store and

has to work. He won't be home until late," Moira said, her perfect even features showing annoyance. "We get one evening out and he has to work the next one. Sometimes it makes me tired!"

"Paul's the one to be tired since he's doing the work," Judy reminded her. "You should be happy to have such an easy life. Hardly any housework, a minimum of cooking and no youngsters to take care of."

Moira pouted. "Now don't start that. You know Paul and I want a family."

"I know Paul does," Judy said, "I can't make my mind up about you."

"You're just being mean now," her sister said. "And there's no need to be jealous. Miles can give you everything that Paul has given me and more. He'd make a wonderful husband."

"If you're so enthusiastic why didn't you marry him?"

Moira stared across the lawn wistfully. "Sometimes I think I should have."

"I gather that by the way you act when he's around," Judy told her. "I think you should be more considerate of Paul."

Moira curled her legs up under her and leaning on an elbow, smiled at Judy lazily like a spoiled kitten. "Paul enjoys being jealous of me," she said, with satisfaction.

"And you enjoy it as well," Judy said with a despairing shake of her head. "I'm glad I'm not the beauty of the family. I don't have your gift for making it pay."

Moira laughed. "You'd better make up your mind about Miles. I don't want an old maid sister."

Judy got up. "I think I might like the idea. We've got a fair quota of old maids among our nursing staff and a lot of them get more fun out of life than some of the sour married ones who come back to work."

"I don't think you should get married just for the sake of being a bride," Moira said. "But when you turn your back on someone like Miles Small, you're wasting a lot of man."

"I'll keep that in mind," Judy said dryly, starting for the house.

"I hadn't planned to get any regular dinner since Paul isn't coming home," her sister called after her. "But there is plenty of everything in the refrigerator. Help yourself!"

Judy went on inside, half-amused and half-annoyed at Moira's talk. The worst part about it was that she knew her attractive sister meant everything she had said. Moira did consider Miles the best catch in Bedford and was more than a little infatuated with him herself even at this late date. Although, when it came right down to it, she was positive Moira would never be unfaithful to Paul. For all her taking him for granted, she really loved him.

It worried Judy that Paul didn't fully realize that. And it was one of the reasons she'd hoped Moira might have a baby. It would serve to bring them closer together and perhaps would also help change the lovely brunette from a flighty charm girl to a devoted mother and wife. Meanwhile, the tension between the young married couple continued.

The next few days passed by without anything really exciting happening. Judy had not had a chance for a confidential chat with Miles since the luncheon they'd had together the day of Mrs. Pomeroy's operation, so she had no way of knowing whether any talk had spread about Dr. Holland's spell at the operating table. Miles had expected Dr. Granger to gossip about the unfortunate incident and he could have very well done so.

There was a sort of quiet about the hospital that might well be the signal of a storm about to break. Dr. Randall had been in to see his patient and had admitted another one, a man with a serious stomach ulcer

91

condition. He had also asked permission for her to scrub for him on Wednesday and Head Nurse Raymond had reluctantly agreed. Judy had an idea the determined young surgeon was going to make a name for himself at Bedford City Hospital. He and Dr. Holland had never been on the floor together so she had yet to discover if they were on better terms.

Mike Conroy, the amputation case, was allowed to go home. Although he was able to walk reasonably well on his crutches, Judy wheeled him to the elevator and then took him to the side entrance where his wife was waiting for him with the family car.

The former postman raised himself from the wheelchair and Judy helped him with his crutches. He walked proudly over to the automobile and with a small assist from her and his wife, slid into the front seat.

"I'll be managing this on my own in no time," he smiled at Judy after the car door was closed.

She leaned with a hand on the window to talk to him. "Promise you'll come back and give us a demonstration after you've mastered that fancy new leg," she said.

"It's a promise," he declared as his wife started the car engine.

Back inside, she had to wait for the elevator. Suddenly she heard a familiar male voice behind her in urgent conversation with another man. At first she did not catch what they were saying, but when she recognized the familiar voice as belonging to Dr. Granger, she began to listen more closely.

"He's losing his grip," Granger was saying in a low angry voice. "The other morning proved that for me. Ask Grant if you like. And now this feud he's carrying on with the new man, Randall, about the use of the O.R. It's nothing more than spite!"

The other voice said something in a low tone to Dr. Granger and then the two moved on out to the other part of the lobby. Judy was tempted to leave the wheelchair standing unattended by the elevator and walk after them to catch the rest of the conversation. Of course she couldn't do it and the elevator arrived at that moment so she took it. But she felt frustrated at having heard so little of what had been said.

At any rate she had learned two things. Dr. Granger was behaving just as Miles had expected. He was deliberately trying to undermine the position of the veteran head of the hospital by spreading the news of his difficulty at the operating table. And the feud between Dr. Holland and Dr. Randall was still going on. This, she felt, was also bad.

She made up her mind to see Miles alone when she had a chance and see if he could bring her up-to-date on the latest developments.

Back on the surgical floor, she had a hard time keeping her mind on her work. She was still worrying about what she'd heard and wondering just how much significance it might have.

One encouraging thing was the splendid progress Calvin Ames was making in recovering from the removal of the malignant tumor from his lung. He was still weak but in good spirits. Judy knew the reports from the lab had been encouraging and Dr. Holland felt there was every reason to believe they had caught the cancer before it had spread to any of the adjoining areas.

It was about an hour later when Dr. Holland made his first visit of the day to the surgical floor. She met him in the corridor and was pleased to see the old man was carrying himself in the same alert way and when he paused to speak with her, it seemed his stern face looked less gaunt.

"How is Mrs. Pomeroy today?" he asked, inquiring about the gall bladder patient.

"She's very uneasy, Doctor," Judy admitted. "But perhaps that is a sign she's no longer as ill as she was." Judy meant that it could indicate she was feeling enough better to be wanting liquor again.

Dr. Holland frowned. "I hope we're not going to have any more problems with her," he said. "Has Dr. Grant been in lately?"

"This morning. He seemed puzzled by her chart. She's running some temperature."

Dr. Holland nodded. "I'll take a look at her," he said, and he went off down the corridor, his step just a trifle less jaunty.

It must have been about twenty minutes later that he came by the nurses' station on his way to the elevator. He stopped to discuss Mrs. Pomeroy's case with Mrs. Raymond asking that certain extra checks be kept on the patient during the next twenty-four hours and the records be sent down to his office. Gallant Bess took his instructions with the air of a martyr who had suffered so much it didn't matter anymore.

After leaving the head nurse, he went directly over to Judy who had been standing by the window only a few feet away. He was frowning slightly as he said, "I understand you are supposed to scrub for Dr. Randall on Wednesday morning?"

She nodded. "Yes. I believe he found himself short a scrub nurse."

Dr. Graham Holland's bulldog face was

95

grimly determined. "You won't be able to," he said. "I'll be needing you in the main operating room."

Judy was startled. "But it has already been arranged, Doctor."

The old man took her surprise quite calmly. "I'll let him know you are not available Wednesday," he said, and continued on to the elevator.

CHAPTER SIX

The elevator closed on the commanding figure of the old surgeon and Head Nurse Raymond came up beside Judy with an angry expression on her face.

"A lot of consideration he shows for anyone," the big woman fumed. "It will take a nurse almost full time for the next twenty-four hours to gather the information he wants on Mrs. Pomeroy! She's been a nuisance from the moment Dr. Grant entered her."

Judy gave her a reproving look. "She is a very sick woman and she hasn't shown the proper response since her operation."

"Let the night shift worry about her," Mrs. Raymond observed sourly.

She had only about twenty minutes more to work and went to Mrs. Pomeroy's room to begin the first of the hourly checks that Dr. Holland had insisted upon. The big woman was very still in her bed and her small eyes barely turned her way when Judy entered.

Judy went over to the bed and prepared for a temperature check. She smiled at the woman and asked, "How are you feeling today?"

Mrs. Pomeroy's answer was brief but emphatic. "Awful!" she moaned.

"You'll feel better soon," Judy assured her.

"I've been hearing that ever since I came here." Her tone was filled with misery and disgust.

Because Judy knew the woman had a right to feel better, she didn't bother to argue the point but went about her duties as quickly and efficiently as she could. But she left with the distinct impression Mrs. Pomeroy was very ill.

She was worried about this development. Aside from the episode of Dr. Holland's seeming dizzy spell, the operation had seemed to go very well. It was hard to understand why Mrs. Pomeroy wasn't doing better. Judy had the thought that it might be because the owner of Bedford's largest florist business had so undermined her health with excessive drinking. No doubt Dr. Holland would soon solve the mystery. This series of tests he was insisting on would go a long way toward doing it.

But she was also upset about the surgeon himself. He had shocked her when he told her she wouldn't be able to scrub for Dr. Randall. She was sure he was deliberately pretending need of her so she couldn't work for the younger man. The gossip around the hospital indicated he had been purposely making it difficult for Dr. Randall. This sort of behavior was so foreign to the head of the hospital that she could hardly accept it. Yet he had been almost sullen when he'd spoken to her about the problem now and he hadn't waited to give her any chance to protest.

Mary Sullivan was waiting for her when she went to change. They had planned to go to the sale at the Avon Department Store. They enjoyed these shopping excursions and on such afternoons Judy preferred to stay in the city and have her dinner with Mary at one of the downtown restaurants.

It turned out there was little to interest them in the sale. But they had the fun of going through the well-stocked store pricing various items. Judy bought only some stockings and a straw Italian sun hat. Mary found a summer dress she liked and that fitted her. Pleased with their purchases, they left the department store early and made their way to a French restaurant on a side street nearby to enjoy dinner.

They both ordered filet of sole and then

relaxed in the quiet booth of the discreetly lighted little restaurant to have a talk. They were usually too busy at the hospital to exchange more than a few words.

"You know the hospital is fairly buzzing with gossip," was Mary's excited opener as she helped herself to a roll from the basket of special breads.

"Isn't it usually?" Judy asked with a weary smile.

"But this is different," Mary said. "Most of the talk is about our own staff. Or to say it plainly, about Dr. Holland."

"I think that's dreadful," Judy protested. "Why do they want to pick on that poor old man who has given his life to the hospital?"

Mary made a face. "You know what people are like. Someone starts a story and then the next one adds something to it. It's mostly about the bad feelings between him and the new surgeon Randall."

"They're likely making too much of it," Judy said, although she couldn't forget that only a couple of hours ago the old surgeon had irritably forbidden her to scrub for Randall. Mary clearly hadn't heard about that yet and Judy didn't think she would mention it. Things were bad enough now.

Mary pondered her remark. "Maybe. But I wouldn't be too certain. They say Dr. Holland isn't himself at all. He had some argument with Mrs. Mason in X-ray. Complained that her department is turning out poor plates. Of course she denied it and there is bad feelings there."

Judy frowned. "I think Dr. Holland is worn out from too much work."

"That's another thing," Mary went on. "The anesthetist, Dr. Granger, is going around telling everyone that Dr. Holland nearly collapsed in O.R. the other day." She gave her an eager look. "I know you were there. Did you see it happen?"

"I did not," she answered with annoyance, "because it didn't happen. He hesitated for a moment during the operation. He told me later he'd gotten something in his eye and it had bothered him."

"Oh!" Mary seemed disappointed. "I thought it would be terribly dramatic."

She said, "Let's talk about something else. You know how I am where Dr. Holland is concerned."

Mary nodded sympathetically. "I'm sorry. Of course, you're right." And at once she changed the subject to clothes, what they might be doing later in the summer, and the problems that had confronted the committee the night of the benefit dance. Their dinner was served and the time passed quickly. It was eight o'clock when she dropped Mary off at her place and drove on to Redmond Acres. When she drew close to the big colonial house she was startled to see Miles Small's car parked on the street in front. She swung into the driveway and quickly parked her own little car and hurried into the house.

At first, she thought no one was inside; then she stepped into the living room and discovered Paul standing staring glumly out the rear window. He was in light slacks and fawn sport shirt open at the neck. He turned as she came in with a resigned expression on his good-looking face.

"Heaven's gift to medicine has been looking for you," Paul said. He nodded to the window, "And right now he's out there entertaining my wife with his wit and humor."

Judy saw that Paul was annoyed again and tried to pass it off lightly. "Why aren't you out there protecting her?"

He shrugged. "I don't think Moira would approve. I'm almost certain she prefers his company to mine."

She touched his arm. "Now you're being silly!"

"I wonder," he said. "She knew Small before she met me and I sometimes think she wishes she had married him."

"That proves you don't know Moira," Judy said. "I'll leave these things upstairs and then I'll go down and see what it's all about."

"Don't rush," he called after her. "Moira is having a wonderful time. It would be a shame to cut it short."

She had an idea it was the turn of events at the hospital that had brought Miles to see her. But she wished he had spoken to her while she was at work and they could have arranged a meeting without sending Paul into one of his jealous moods. Remembering the young surgeon's eagerness to get Moira to himself at the dance, she realized Miles might have deliberately arranged it so he would have an excuse to come here looking for her and spend some time with her sister.

Paul was certain he had grounds for jealousy and perhaps he had. The friendship that once existed between the two men had vanished and she blamed it mostly on Miles. Of course, Moira also shared some of the responsibility. She could do things to anger Paul without realizing it and she did like to flirt.

This fact was underlined when Judy went out onto the back lawn to discover Miles and her sister sitting close together on the hammock in deep conversation. Moira wasn't in her brief outfit of the other afternoon, which was a small blessing, but she was wearing a sun suit in black and orange polka-dots with a daring low top and thin, almost invisible, shoulder straps that made Judy feel drab in her plain fawn linen.

Moira saw her first and with a smile, said, "Here you are at last! Miles has been frantic to see you!"

Judy gave the two a derisive smile. "I'd say he had settled down pretty well."

Miles gave Moira an amused glance. "I thank you for one thing, Moira. I think you've finally made her jealous." He came over to Judy.

"Oh, no," Moira protested with an innocence to match her fresh beauty. "We've never been jealous of each other. Not even when we were just youngsters."

"That's true," Judy agreed. "We always shared everything. I don't think Moira realizes we've passed that time now." She gave her sister a meaningful look. "Paul was looking for you."

Moira took the hint. "Oh, really? I must go see what he wants." She got up from the hammock and with a farewell smile for the young surgeon, said, "Do come over soon again, Miles!"

"Depend on it," he said, with a return smile. When she had gone he turned to Judy and told her, "I'm glad you finally arrived."

She gave him a teasing appraisal. "I wonder. You and Moira seemed to be enjoying yourselves."

"But I didn't come to see her."

"I wonder about that, too!"

He raised a hand. "Honest injun!" he said. "I intended to speak to you at the hospital and ask you about tonight but you were off somewhere busy when I was on your floor."

"What about tonight?" she asked.

"I want you to come over to Dr. Holland's place with me," he said.

Her big brown eyes opened wide. "What is it all about?"

"A number of things," he said. "Let's get on our way or we'll be late. I can tell you in the car."

Judy was uncertain and not a little flustered. "I'm not dressed for paying a call," she protested.

"You look fine to me," he said, taking her gently by the arm and leading her around to the front of the house and his car.

She might have refused to go had she not known of the chaotic conditions at the hospital. She had no doubt his visit to the old surgeon tonight had some bearing on the gossip that was being so carelessly bandied around, and she decided she might as well find out any facts he might have. When they were in the car and driving to Dr. Holland's she began to question him.

"Has your visit any bearing on the stories going around about him?" she wanted to know.

Miles nodded, keeping his eyes on the road. "In a sense. My excuse is the Student Nurses Society is having a raffle to raise extra money for their graduation dance. Dr. Holland has offered to donate one of his paintings for the purpose and the girls asked me to select it. I thought I'd bring you along to get the woman's viewpoint."

"Sounds like a pleasant task," she said happily. "The two paintings in his office are good. I wonder if his other work measures up to that standard."

"I have been told he's got real talent," Miles said. "I've never been to his place before, so this will be the first time for both of us."

Judy didn't question this because she knew that Dr. Holland rarely entertained guests. He probably wouldn't be seeing them now except that their visit had a bearing on the hospital.

"I understand he has a large old house,"

Judy said. "Isn't it on Lorne Row?"

"Yes. It's about the last of the private homes in that district," the young surgeon agreed. "Most of the other ones have been converted into small apartments. The district has gone down a good deal since he bought there." He paused. "Of course, Granger made good on my prediction and has spread it all over the hospital he thinks the old man is on the point of collapse."

"But that's so unfair," Judy said with a frown. "So are all the other rumors they're spreading."

The handsome young surgeon looked worried as he halted the car for a red light. He looked at her and said, "You know I'm on his side."

"Yet, we must face it. He is to blame for some of his troubles."

Miles asked, "What do you mean?"

"Face facts," she said quietly. "Dr. Holland has been carrying on a feud with the X-ray people lately, claiming they're turning out fuzzy plates."

"Sometimes they do."

"Not often," Judy said, as the car started again and they moved on into the main flow of traffic.

Miles kept busy at the wheel. "So you think he's unfair."

"He's growing old and crotchety. That explains it."

"That's not the kind of loyalty I expected from you."

She gave the young man a searching glance and then stared at the road ahead. "Aren't you allowing hero-worship to warp your judgment?"

He sighed. "That could be. Perhaps it's because he has become a true father figure to me. I have never been able to identify with my own father. I grew up hating the world of politics, and medicine has been a refuge for me, with Dr. Holland my idol."

"You shouldn't carry it too far," she said. "Dr. Holland has his share of faults. He's gone out of his way to make it difficult for John Randall."

"If I'm forced to take sides, I'll have to take Dr. Holland's."

Judy said, "I know. But there are a lot of bad feelings building up at the hospital. You may soon be forced to declare yourself. You've said the board feels Holland is holding them back with their improvement plan, and Randall has accused him of making operating facilities hard for him to come by. Now the latest is the old man has preempted the main operating room for Wednesday even though Randall had already spoken for it. So Randall is left with the smaller room and skeleton staff."

"I've heard the entire story from both sides," Miles admitted. "Dr. Holland spoke to me first, and he mentioned you'd be scrubbing for him rather than for Randall."

"There you are!" Judy said sharply. "Don't you call that unfair?"

"Again I'll defer judgment," Miles said. "That's the way I feel. I have to. In all the years I've worked with Dr. Holland, he has always been just."

"Suppose he is jealous of John Randall?"

"That's completely ridiculous!" Miles protested. "Randall hasn't even started to operate at Bedford City yet."

"He brings an impressive reputation with him from St. Mary's," she said. "He has been in the city only a year and they regard him as their top surgeon over there. They're heartbroken at his coming to us."

"Coming to us because he respects the very standards that Graham Holland has created," Miles said.

Judy smiled at this. "You're right," she agreed, "but doesn't it make the situation all the more tragic? When Randall does that ileostomy Wednesday it will be the first time any doctor other than Dr. Holland has done one at the hospital. When he hasn't done them they've always gone to Boston, and frankly, I think the old man is jealous."

"I can't condemn him so matter-of-factly," Miles said stubbornly. "I'll admit he's unwell and perhaps confused, but that is all!"

They had come to a side street with a sign "Lorne Row" and Miles swung the car into it. "Somehow I've got to warn him," he said. "Things are coming to a head and the rumors Granger is spreading aren't helping."

Judy shook her head in despair. "Mary told me they're saying he collapsed at the operating table."

"This kind of story always snowballs," Miles said as he pulled the car to the curb beside a rambling, brown three-story house. It was built in the style of thirty years earlier but Judy could see it had been kept up well. There was still some daylight, although the sun was sinking rapidly, and they were able to enjoy the flower gardens in front and to the side of the house as they made their way to the front door.

A pleasant elderly woman came in answer to the doorbell and showed them into the cool dark hallway. "Dr. Holland is expecting you," she told them. "He said to go right out to the veranda. Just follow the hallway."

They did. Judy was struck by the general atmosphere of the old house. It reflected the character of the fine old man who lived in it, a man she didn't like to hear being gossiped about by the hospital crowd. At the end of the hall, a doorway opened directly onto a big glassed-in back veranda. It was here they found Graham Holland, brush in hand, seated on a tall stool facing an easel which held a large, unfinished canvas of a seascape.

As soon as he saw them he got down from the stool and came forward with a smile. "Glad you came, Miles," he said. And beaming at Judy, he said, "Nice you could join him, Miss Scott. I don't generally have such pretty guests."

She felt her cheeks warm to his compliment, and stepping forward, she studied the painting. "It's the Point," she said, glancing around at the old man with a smile of delighted recognition. "I could tell it right away."

Miles stepped forward to examine it. "I like your style," he said.

"Nothing great," the old man said with commendable modesty. "I just try to put down with simple strokes what I see. It takes a surgeon's eyesight, I can tell you that. And a reasonably steady hand."

"You should have plenty of training then," Miles laughed. "What do you plan to let the girls have?"

The old man waved his hand toward the house. "We'll go into my gallery and you can take your pick. I promised they could have any one of them."

He escorted them to the gallery, a large room with walls lined with paintings. He stopped and told something about each canvas. Judy liked his use of bright colors and felt his seascapes were the best. On this point Miles agreed, and a large painting of a storm-lashed beach was the one they selected for the student nurses' raffle. Afterward, the old surgeon insisted they join him in his study for coffee and cake.

The study was a friendly, medium-sized room with bookshelves on three walls. The old man sat at his desk while Judy and Miles faced him in black leather easy chairs of ancient vintage.

"This is the other half of my life," Dr. Holland said. "My painting has allowed me to go on living happily in this lonely house."

Judy recalled the story she had heard of the little girl who had died of meningitis and the adored wife who had turned against his dedication to medicine and left him, taking their only other child with her and never returning. She felt sorry for him and doubly upset at the trouble he must surely sense he was facing at the hospital.

"Your painting will give you something to work with when you retire," Miles told the senior surgeon.

Dr. Holland's lined face showed sadness. "When I am too decrepit to wield a scalpel I'll be too shaky to do anything with a paint brush."

He'll not give in easily, Judy thought. It will be a battle before they take everything from him. He'll offer them a good fight.

"I doubt if the board will ever accept your retirement as head of the surgical staff," Miles said with a smile, including Judy in his glance. She noticed that he had been careful to refer only to the old man's position as head surgeon, diplomatically leaving out any reference to his role of head of the hospital.

Apparently Graham Holland had also noted this delicate handling of a touchy subject. He smiled and said, "I had a stormy meeting with the board, you know. I have the feeling they're not satisfied with my stand on the new improvements."

"Is it worth your while to battle with them?" Miles asked. "Wouldn't you be better off to allow someone else to take over administration and devote yourself fully to your surgical work?"

The old man looked slightly startled at this. "You're speaking plainly enough, young man."

"I'm thinking of you, sir, and I'd like to see your strength conserved so you can devote yourself where you are needed most — in the operating room."

Dr. Holland nodded. "It's a valid argument and I may give it some thought one day soon." His face became grim. "But I'll not let the likes of Dr. Granger and his vultures force me." He paused. "You know that Granger has been playing politics to see if he can become my successor! Having failed as a doctor, he's not satisfied to have a protected spot as our anesthetist. He wants to run the whole hospital!"

Judy gave Miles a meaningful glance. "So that's it," she said softly.

"I'll not retire and let that sort of leadership take over," Dr. Holland said in his harsh voice. "Not if I break myself fighting them."

Miles seemed startled and depressed. He stared down at the rug. "I hope it won't come to that, sir," he said quietly.

"And we have new men who want to show us their talents as well," the senior surgeon said angrily, "young men who have made quick reputations and expect to come into our hospital and run it as they see fit." He paused. "I think you both know I'm referring to Dr. John Randall."

"In fairness, sir," Miles said respectfully, "he has made a good name for himself since coming to the city. They thought highly of him at St. Mary's."

"I am not head of staff at St. Mary's," Dr. Holland reminded him. "I have found Dr. Randall sullen and stubborn in my dealings with him. Both traits I dislike finding in a medical man, especially in a surgeon."

Judy knew she was talking a chance, but could not resist asking, "Is that why you have opposed him, Doctor?"

"Whatever I have done," the old man said slowly, "has been in the best interests of our profession." He hesitated and then added, "And I would hope in his best interests as well."

CHAPTER SEVEN

They stayed a while longer with Dr. Holland but the discussion switched back to art and the old surgeon displayed a tremendous knowledge of the field. It was close to midnight before Judy and Miles left. The evening in the gallant old surgeon's company had left them both thoughtful, and neither of them had much to say until the car was heading along the main street again.

Miles spoke in the semi-darkness of the front seat, his handsome, aristocratic face barely visible in the reflection from the dash lights. "Do you still feel the same way about him?" he asked.

Judy glanced across at him. "Yes. He believes he's doing right; give him credit for that. Let's hope that's the way it turns out."

"I've been thinking," the young surgeon said. "It can get very lonely at the top."

Judy braced herself against the seat angrily. "What really makes me rage is that weasel Granger. Of course that's why he's spread his malicious stories. He actually thinks he might get the board to vote him head of the hospital."

"Stranger things have happened," Miles said as he drove around a traffic circle, "or perhaps I should say things equally as bad. He may have one or two friends on the board he can count as giving him support. That makes it just a matter of swinging a few others his way and he's in."

"You must get your father to stand up for Dr. Holland. He is bound to have a lot of influence on the board."

He gave her a wry smile. "I've tried to keep out of hospital politics. Maybe Dad's being on the board did have something to do with my appointment to the staff in the first place, but I've been determined to stand on my merits as a doctor ever since. I've never interfered with hospital policies and I don't know that I want to now."

"This is not for yourself," she pointed out. "It's for Dr. Holland."

"I'll think about it," he promised moodily.

"I'm more worried about his health than anything else," Judy said. "If he keeps well, he will be more than a match for them. But there's something about him that worries me, I mean aside from what happened those times in the operating room. I seem to sense he's not as well as he tries to pretend."

"I know what you mean," Miles agreed,

as if he might have had the same idea. "What do you think of his attitude towards Randall?"

Judy looked out the side window of the car, staring at the street lights. "I'm going to surprise you," she said. "I don't think he is as opposed to John Randall as he'd like to have us believe."

He said, "You do surprise me and I can't see what you're getting at."

"I'll go out on a limb and say I think he is more worried about Dr. Randall becoming too sure and satisfied before he has had proper experience than he is of any possible competition from him."

"And all this dueling with him is simply to keep him in his proper place until Holland is convinced he warrants the adulation he's already getting."

"Yes," she said. "I think it's a protective measure on the old man's part. He may see Randall as someone much like himself when he was young. For that reason, he's anxious to have him build solidly."

Miles was derisive. "The way he's attacking him now there won't be any building at all. It's my guess Randall will resign and go back to St. Mary's unless the old man goes easier on him."

"Maybe that is what he wants to find

out," Judy said thoughtfully. "He is testing him to discover just how much he can take."

They were back in Redmond Acres now, parked before the big white colonial house. Miles turned to her with a smile. "I hope you'll soon decide you've had enough hospital and give me some consideration."

She offered a wan smile of her own. "If things keep on as they are, that might happen sooner than you think."

"Great," he said. "I should do all I can to make them worse."

She laughed. "Don't try that! I'll remember what you said."

He pretended regret. "I'm always much too frank for my own good," he sighed.

He saw her to the door and she thought his goodnight kiss was just a trifle more sincere and tender than any he had given her before. In the moment of his embrace she began to feel more certain it was her and not Moira he truly loved.

She went upstairs in the midnight quiet of the big house and began to prepare for bed, but she lay awake for a long time considering the evening just ended and what it might eventually mean. It seemed certain that events at the hospital were bound to take a turn for the worse before they improved. She hoped that her plea to Miles to invoke his father's aid on Dr. Holland's behalf might produce some good results. Brandon Small undoubtedly had the prestige to make the board listen to his views and probably he could swing many of its members to vote along with him in any dispute.

But no amount of political maneuvering would assist the old surgeon if his health collapsed. She had been almost sure she had noticed a slight tremble in his hand as he'd passed her cup and saucer to her. A weakness she had never noticed before and one that could be the beginning of the end for any surgeon. She had not even mentioned it to Miles, but from now on she would watch closely.

As for the hostility between Dr. Holland and Dr. Randall, she was again somewhat confused. While the old surgeon had made it plain he resented the way Randall expected to come into the hospital and have everything made easily available to him, there was also a hint of something else in his attitude, something of the harsh discipline of an old craftsman for a promising apprentice. And if Dr. Holland really saw the young surgeon in that light, no one need have any fears about his future. Judy was banking heavily that she was right in this judgment. She pictured the earnest face of John Randall and then thought of the old man who had talked so gravely to them from behind his desk tonight and it struck her they were much alike in many ways. This was her last waking thought.

The surgical floor was as busy as ever the next day. Head Nurse Raymond was in a particularly vindictive mood because she had been forced to take over the remaining hours of the exhaustive testing Dr. Holland was demanding in Mrs. Pomeroy's case. She vented her wrath for being responsible for this extra work on all her staff. Judy found herself doing most of the tests and carefully setting down the results that the senior surgeon was waiting for.

She was baffled by Mrs. Pomeroy's continued pain and lack of general recovery. Having been a member of the operating team, she took a particular interest in the case, and Mrs. Raymond did not miss a chance to remind her sarcastically that she had assisted in the operation.

"What did you people do to her down there?" the head nurse asked with a faint sneer as Judy paused to jot some information down on Mrs. Pomeroy's chart. "I've never seen a patient take this long to get over a gall bladder operation."

Judy ignored the taunt and looked up with her pretty, young face shadowed. "There must be something else wrong with her," she said. "There has to be."

"Well, she's awfully dry, we know that," Mrs. Raymond observed with irony. "Maybe if you gave her that half-bottle of whiskey we still have in her briefcase she'd snap out of it."

Judy smiled ruefully. "The idea is tempting but I don't think it would really do any good. She must have some other physical trouble the doctor doesn't know about. Something that is complicating her present condition."

The head nurse waved scornfully at the records Judy was preparing. "He's got enough data there to feed a computer for a month. What's he going to do with it?"

"Some detective work to try and discover what is really wrong."

"I know what I'd like to do," the head nurse said darkly. "I'd like to dress her, give her that briefcase with what's in it and send her packing!"

So it went on all morning. Miles came by about eleven-thirty and looked in on Mrs. Pomeroy. Afterward, he consulted Judy about the charts and studied them with a baffled expression.

"I don't know what the old man will say when he sees these temperature recordings," he observed with a frown. "But I'd say the patient is in serious trouble and so are we."

"What can be wrong?" Judy said.

The young surgeon rubbed his left temple as he pondered. "Could be some chronic liver trouble that has suddenly flared up after the operation."

"She's a prime candidate for cirrhosis."

"Granted," he agreed. "With all her record of drinking it's almost too easy a diagnosis."

"What else?"

He shook his head. "Failure somewhere along the line. I'll leave this one to Dr. Holland to guess. It's the first case of his to give trouble in ages. He should be able to figure the answer."

So that was where it stood. Among the other doctors who showed on the surgical floor were Dr. Randall and Dr. Granger. Dr. Randall came first and seemed in a great hurry. He didn't stop to talk with Judy, but he did nod and give her a faint smile. She was so pleased with the smile she forgave him for his rush, knowing that he was undoubtedly pushed for time. Dr. Granger arrived later and was in a more leisurely mood, and as Judy suspected, he was looking for information. The head nurse was busy at the phone when he arrived so he sidled up to bother Judy.

He offered his nervous smile and she thought it made him seem even more weasel-like. Then he said, "So we meet again, Miss Scott. This is your domain?"

"I work on this floor most of the time," she said with cool politeness.

He was no taller than she was and he stood with his balding head slightly forward, an oily smile on his pointed features and his hands clasped behind his back. Judy had liked most of the anesthetists she'd met and had found them all careful, highly-skilled men and women. But she couldn't include Dr. Granger in the group. She had often wondered why Dr. Holland had been so sharp with the little man during operations and why he had checked him so often and taken really unusual precautions. Last night the old man had revealed the truth. He knew Granger to be a second-rate doctor and had been taking pains to see he made no mistakes.

Now Dr. Granger eyed her slyly. "Of course, you are also a part of the great man's O.R. team a good deal of the time."

"I scrub for Dr. Holland occasionally."

"It seems we've met down there a good deal," he said. "Are you working with him tomorrow?"

"Yes, I believe I am."

The oily smile appeared again. "I have been demoted to the other operating room and assisting the new man, Randall," Dr. Granger said, "I believe Dr. Hunter is taking my place. You are very lucky to remain in favor with the head."

"I don't think it's a question of that," she said, growing more angry.

"Dr. Holland has his pets and his tantrums as well." Dr. Granger glanced up and down the corridor as if he were afraid someone might be listening to him and then the bald head bent closer to her. "I can tell you things are apt to change soon around here. Many people think Dr. Holland is breaking up."

"So I've heard," she said icily.

But he took no warning from her tone. "You must have seen what happened in the operating room. How he slumped over the patient." He paused. "And I understand she hasn't been doing well. Making a very slow recovery, eh?"

"If you want any information about Mrs. Pomeroy I suggest you talk to Dr. Holland," she said. "And as for predicted changes and wild rumors, I have no interest in hearing your versions of them." With that she walked away leaving him open-mouthed.

At lunch, Mary Sullivan queried her about the episode. The two girls were sharing a table together. Mary asked, "What did you do to old Granger?"

Judy couldn't help smiling. "Why?"

"I saw you walking away from him and when I came up to the nurses' station he glared at me as if I'd offended him. Then he went straight to Gallant Bess and began to pour out some tale of woe about you being insulting to him."

Judy looked complacent. "And what did dear Head Nurse Raymond say to that?"

Mary laughed. "She was in a bad mood of her own and didn't give him much encouragement. She told him not to worry about being an exception because you insulted everyone regularly and her most of all."

"That must have really pleased him!"

"He hit the ceiling all right and started accusing Gallant Bess of not having proper respect for a doctor and of encouraging her floor nurses to have no respect as well. Her answer to that one was she wasn't certain an anesthetist should be regarded as a member of the medical profession since most of the good ones she knew were nurses like herself and that, in fact, she had been an anesthetist when he was likely flunking in medical school."

Judy now was forced to join in her friend's laughter. "She must have been at her best!"

"She was," Mary assured her. "He walked off like a frustrated little rooster and promised to report her and everyone else on the floor."

"To whom?" Judy wanted to know. "I'm sure Dr. Holland won't listen to him, and everyone else in the hospital knows Granger has been going around trying to create trouble."

"Just the same, he'll have it in for you," Mary warned. "And you have got a reputation for talking back. So, tread softly, Nurse Scott! You've been told that a time or two before."

Of course, Head Nurse Raymond wasn't going to let her get off without a mention of her indiscretion. She was waiting for Judy when she got off the elevator after lunch.

"Are you getting tired of the hospital, Miss Scott?" was her sweetly put opening question.

"I don't understand," she said, trying hard not to laugh.

The woman scowled at her. "I know you do. So don't play pure little Polly for my benefit. You insulted Dr. Granger and he was furious!"

"Oh, that!" Judy said. "I promise I'll gladly take full responsibility for anything I said."

Head Nurse Raymond glared around at some of the other nurses, including Mary Sullivan, who had lingered at the nurses' station to hear the fun and said, "Dr. Granger seems to feel I am responsible for the conduct of all the nurses on the floor. I told him I tried to be and it wasn't my fault if most of them happened to be a little odd. I have a theory the nursing supervisor sends all her misfits up here because I happen to have experience."

It could have gone on endlessly, but Judy saved herself by glancing up and saying, "The light in 423 is on. I'd better go see what's wrong with Mrs. Pomeroy."

Mrs. Raymond gave her a glance of scathing contempt. "That's all you're fit to look after," she snapped. "Drunks!"

Judy was still inwardly chuckling as she walked down the corridor, but when she went in and saw the state Mrs. Pomeroy was in, she lost all her merriment. The big woman was tossing restlessly and her small eyes looked up at her imploringly.

"I feel a lot worse. More pain," Mrs.

Pomeroy moaned. "Get the doctor."

Judy lingered only a moment to make Mrs. Pomeroy as comfortable as possible and then rushed back to the nurses' station and told the head nurse about the situation. Mrs. Raymond was still in her mood and it was with ponderous reluctance that she sat down to phone Dr. Holland. As it turned out, the senior surgeon was not available, but she did reach Miles and he promised to come right up.

When Miles arrived, he explained that Dr. Holland had been called on to assist as consultant with a major operation being performed at St. Mary's and he would be gone most of the afternoon.

He eyed Judy worriedly as they made their way down the corridor. "Is she really a lot worse?"

"I'm afraid so," she said. "And I think her jaundice has returned."

Miles groaned. "This would be the afternoon Holland would be away."

He examined Mrs. Pomeroy and talked to her in gentle tones explaining that Dr. Holland would see her as soon as he returned, but she seemed to be too ill to be much interested any longer. He ordered that she be given a mild sedative to settle her restlessness and pain until Dr. Holland could see her. He also collected the charts Judy had prepared and took them down so they would be immediately available to show the senior surgeon when he came back from St. Mary's.

Dr. Randall's patient in 439 seemed to be getting panicky as the morning of her operation came closer. All in all it was a trying afternoon. Between keeping a close watch on Mrs. Pomeroy, doing routine chores for other patients, and trying to placate the nervous Gertrude Miller, Judy was kept on the run.

Mrs. Miller kept asking questions in an apparent attempt to keep her in the room. She couldn't seem to endure being alone. She wanted to know everything about the operation. "How long will it take?" she asked, not aware this was the standard query of almost every surgical patient.

Judy struggled to be patient and understanding. "Not more than an hour," she said.

Gertrude Miller's small face showed new fear. "Isn't that a very long time to be in there?" she asked.

"Not really," Judy assured her. "Some operations take as long as several hours. With the anesthesia used today, it's perfectly safe."

The woman shook her head. "Sometimes I think I'm making a terrible mistake. Dr. Randall is so young. Do you think I'm right to trust him?"

"I would if I were in your place," Judy told her.

The schoolteacher clasped and unclasped her hands nervously and stared at the floor. "I get so upset. I worry that I may never be able to work again."

"But that's nonsense," Judy said. "You'll be perfectly able to work and probably lose less time than you have before because of your illness. You can be thankful this operation has been perfected. In the old days people with serious ulcerative colitis died."

Gertrude Miller's eyebrows raised. "You mean without this operation there really was no cure?"

"That's right," Judy said.

The schoolteacher gave a deep sigh. "I suppose I have been making a great fuss when I should really be thankful, but it is a big step and I've never undergone an operation of any kind before."

Judy smiled. "I understand and you needn't be ashamed of being nervous. Most people are."

She stayed a few minutes longer in 439 and then went back to the nurses' station.

Dr. Holland had not gotten back to the hospital yet, and Mrs. Pomeroy had fallen into a light sleep after being given the medication. At least she would rest easier for awhile.

It wasn't until she reached the house in Redmond Acres that she knew how completely exhausted the difficult day had left her. As she started wearily up the stairs to her room, Moira came out of the living room in her sun dress.

"Don't you want to talk for awhile?" she asked in a disappointed tone. "I've been sitting here waiting for you to come home."

"Sorry," she said. "I'm dead! I'm going to take a short nap and a shower before dinner. I'll see you afterward."

As she went on upstairs she heard Moira mumbling something else to herself as she voiced her disappointment, but Judy didn't care. She was beyond that. As soon as she reached her room, she closed the drapes and threw herself on her bed.

She awoke with a start and realized guiltily she had slept well into the dinner hour. Rising quickly, she went to the bathroom and prepared to take a shower. She knew it would bring her fully awake and make her feel better for the evening meal and the night ahead. She was grateful to Moira for allowing her to sleep on and would make apologies for being so abrupt to her on the way in when she went downstairs.

As the tingling water sprayed her body into a new awareness, she found her thoughts returning to the hospital and what was happening there. She was worried about Mrs. Pomeroy and wondered what Dr. Holland's verdict would be and what he would do. Perhaps it was cirrhosis of the liver as the woman's record of drinking would suggest, but Miles had seemed to be doubtful on this point. Too easy, he had said, and perhaps he was right. She knew that when these difficult problems arose, they were often dreadfully hard to track down.

If Mrs. Pomeroy should get worse rapidly and die, it would certainly give the vindictive little Dr. Granger plenty of ammunition against Dr. Holland. He had more than hinted to her that he considered the senior surgeon had bungled the case. He would undoubtedly he much franker in his denunciation to anyone else. Judy's face was grim with thought as she quickly towelled herself and slipped into fresh underthings and a yellow dress suitable for the evening.

Paul and Moira were at the table when she went into the dining room. "Sorry," she said with a smile. "Overslept again. I can only plead guilty to a bad case of sleeping sickness, I guess."

Paul gave her an understanding smile. "I don't imagine eight long hours in a hot hospital had anything to do with it."

Moira shook her head in despair. "Working herself to skin and bone for a pittance when she could marry Miles and have a lovely home!"

Judy raised a hand to silence her. "No matchmaking until after the main course. I'm too weak to defend myself."

She had just finished her grapefruit when the phone rang. Paul took it and came back to the dining room to say it was for Judy.

Judy rose quickly with a feeling of alarm. Her first thought was that Mrs. Pomeroy had died and this was Miles phoning to tell her the bad news. She hurried out to the hallway to take the call.

But when she lifted the phone and answered it, it wasn't Miles at the other end of the line but someone else, someone whom she had least expected to hear from — Dr. John Randall.

CHAPTER EIGHT

"Sorry to be a nuisance," he said from the other end of the line in his sober way.

"That's all right," she told him.

"I wondered if you were going to be busy later in the evening," the young doctor said. "I have something I'd like to discuss with you."

Judy was immediately on guard. She was certain it was the question of not acting as his scrub nurse in the morning that was on his mind, and while she had the feeling he was not being treated fairly, she could not question Dr. Holland's authority, and Dr. Holland had informed her she would be scrubbing for him rather than Dr. Randall. She hoped the young man would understand her position in the matter.

She hesitated. "Is it something really important? I was going to bed early tonight. I'm to be in the operating room in the morning."

"I realize that," he said, "and I won't keep you out late. But I do think you should hear what I have to say."

"Very well," she said, resigned to an unhappy scene. "What time will you call?"

"I'm in my office now," he said. "I have quite a few patients to see and there'll be more along. But I think I can be free and over there by nine-fifteen at the latest."

"I'll be here," she promised.

"Thanks again," he said. "You'll understand why I felt it had to be tonight when I see you and explain."

She put down the phone with a worried expression on her face. He was bound to question her about switching to Dr. Holland's team. She hoped he wouldn't ask her to take a stand against the old man. If he did, she didn't know what she would say. While Dr. Holland's actions had all the appearance of wrong in this matter, there might be other factors involved unknown to her. She had no wish to take a stand yet.

Back at the dinner table she told Moira the young doctor would be calling for her later. Her sister paused with a spoonful of strawberry dessert poised in the air to register a pleased surprise.

"That's the new fellow," she said. "The one who was at the Benefit Dance. He's very sober and looks a little like Richard Burton. All the women were talking about him."

"Dr. John Randall," Judy confirmed his

name. "I wouldn't say he's all that attractive."

Moira sighed and registered a pensive expression. "He has a certain quality," she said, and then, her mood changing, added, "but I don't think he compares with Miles Small."

"You wouldn't," Paul said with a droll glance her way.

"Now don't make a lot of it, darling!" his wife reproved. "I only meant Miles is much better husband material for Judy."

Paul rolled his eyes and sat back with a sigh. "And how do you measure husband material? By the yard? Do you take the quality and width into consideration along with the texture of the hair? I never heard such crazy talk in all my life."

Moira was pleasantly vague. "You don't see things from a woman's point of view, dear."

"That's pretty obvious," he said, getting up in a mild rage and tossing his napkin on the table. "Is there any reason I should?" He stalked out of the room.

Judy gave her sister a despairing glance. "It seems you always manage to upset him."

Moira shrugged. "He's entirely too touchy. Whenever I mention Miles, he gets in a rage."

"I know, and sometimes I think that's why you insist on bringing him into the conversation — just for the fun of teasing Paul!"

"You have a horrid mind!" Moira said, but she smiled at the same time and in no way denied Judy's accusation.

It was almost dark when John Randall drove up and mounted the steps to ring the front doorbell. Moira was upstairs somewhere and Paul was in the study leaving Judy alone to answer the door.

"Won't you come in?"

He stood there rather shyly. "It's a marvelous night," he said. "I'd hoped you might like to drive to the beach."

Judy smiled. "If that's what you'd like, I'd enjoy it."

"Then why wait?" he said.

When they were in the car and driving along the four-lane highway to the coastal area, he said, "I've only become familiar with a few of the roads, but I think this is the first one I drove on. I like the seashore. I was used to it in California, although the country is different out there."

"It's much more rugged in most places, isn't it?" she said.

He nodded, keeping his eyes fixed ahead. "Great high cliffs and winding roads that follow them. I think it's the most wonderful scenery in the world. I'm planning to go back there one day."

"There are some rugged shore areas in Maine and other of the Northeastern States," Judy said, "but we have mostly sandy beaches here with few rocky sections."

"This kind of place has charm as well," he was willing to admit. It was dark now and the breeze was getting cooler. He had put the headlights on and they were caught in heavy traffic with cars whizzing in both directions.

Soon she could smell the salt tang of the sea as they followed a narrower winding road that went directly along the ocean front. On one side of it there were houses and on the other a low concrete wall and parking areas. Dr. Randall turned the car into a vacant place and brought it to a halt. They were now directly facing the ocean. This was a cove area and far out on the water she could see the colored lights of a marking buoy.

The young surgeon turned to her. "Would you like to walk on the beach?"

"I'd love to," she said.

"It should be pleasant, although it seems a dark night," he said as he got out of the car.

He helped her down the nearby concrete steps that led to the beach. She looked up and saw that there were no stars and only the hazy glow of a hidden moon emerging from heavy clouds. Yet, the night was warm. Quite a few people were gathered in groups on the beach. One such group was seated in a circle around a brisk fire which they had started from gathered driftwood. She thought that later, when it became cooler, they might need it even more.

She and Dr. Randall went far down the beach until they were close to the rolling waves and the continuous wash of them was loud in their ears. His sober face wore a thoughtful expression.

"Nearly everyone has a longing for the sea," he said at last. "I suppose because it was the beginning of things for all of us."

"So I've heard," she said with a small laugh. She was nervous and wished that he would get on with whatever he had to tell her. They began to walk slowly along the beach.

"I guess I must seem like a pretty dull person to you," he said, his head slightly bent as he walked.

"On the contrary," Judy said. "My sister assures me you're one of the most exciting men to come to Bedford. And she's an authority."

"Thank her for me," he said with a touch of humor in his voice. "Comments like that help build a man's ego."

"Most men don't need it," she said.

"I'm one of the exceptions." He paused. "I'm sorry you won't be working with me tomorrow."

"So am I." She was sincere enough in saying this.

He hesitated a moment before speaking again. Then he said, "I don't think it was any accident Dr. Holland scheduled an operation for the main room at the exact time I'd booked it and also discovered he needed vital members of the team I had lined up."

"He has a terribly busy schedule of operations," she reminded him. "I doubt if it was anything more than coincidence."

"I happen to believe he is doing this deliberately," Dr. Randall said. "He didn't want me in the hospital in the first place, and now he is making it as difficult for me as he can."

"Why should he?"

"I suppose he has personal reasons," he said, his tone weary. "And the unpleasant aspect of the whole business is I suspect he's cracking up as a surgeon and as head of the hospital. This is just one sign of it."

Judy glanced at him and saw the angry frustration in his face. "Evidently you've been listening to Dr. Granger and his friends," she said. "I think I should warn you Dr. Granger is looking for the job as head of the hospital himself." She added bitterly, "Of course he isn't capable of it!"

"I know about that too," he said. "If anyone should follow Holland as head of Bedford City it should be Miles Small. Whatever his limitations as a surgeon, he has an easy way with people. He's a natural for executive responsibility."

His words came to her as a surprise because she hadn't really seriously considered Miles for the job. But now she saw that John was right. Miles did have the qualifications to head the hospital. Not only that, but he was well-liked by nearly everyone. In a way she was perhaps the least appreciative of his many close friends. She accepted him as an amusing companion and someone she could rely on, but she also saw him as a flirt and not always as dedicated as he could be in his approach to medicine. For the first time, she stood aloof and considered him and she was surprised at her conclusions. One of them was that she was definitely not in love with him or she could not appraise his qualities in this completely emotionless manner.

John glanced at her. "You haven't offered

an opinion yet? Don't you agree Small would be a logical successor to Dr. Holland?"

Embarrassed at the long silence that must have seemed odd to the man at her side, she nodded. "Yes. I do agree with you on that."

"But you don't think Dr. Holland is on the edge of a breakdown?"

"No. I can't see why you do either." Some indignation had come into her voice.

The young surgeon halted and faced her. She could barely make out his features in the murky light, but she could tell that his expression was deadly serious. "That's the real reason I asked you out here tonight," he said. "I have something to tell you that may change your mind."

"I can't believe that," she warned him.

"Listen to me," he said firmly. "A few months ago I had a patient come to see me at my office. She had been operated on by Dr. Holland a while before. She'd gone to him because it was his specialty, a gall bladder removal. When she came to me, she was ill again and I saw at once she still showed signs of some trouble in that area. On a hunch I decided to send her to a clinic in Boston. Within a week I had their report, and it was interesting. They suggested the woman would require another operation."

"I don't understand," Judy said faintly.

"Neither did I until later," he said. "The woman remained at the Boston hospital and was operated on at once. This was what they advised. The results of the operation were good and the woman recovered. But I was shocked to hear what the trouble had been." He paused. "According to the confidential report sent me, the gall bladder ducts had been badly damaged in the previous operation and had caused the woman's second illness."

"You're saying Dr. Holland bungled the operation," she said incredulously. "But he's been a specialist in this field for years! He must have done a thousand such operations!"

"Perhaps more," John said quietly, "and yet he showed no sign of his skill in this instance. Doesn't that suggest something to you?"

"It suggests that it was a freak case," Judy said. "Every surgeon comes up against one now and then."

"I agree," the young man said with a sigh, "except that two weeks ago when I was in Boston, I talked with the clinic surgeon, and he told me that the case I sent him was the second of that kind he'd seen within a year. The other one had been a patient of Dr.

Holland's as well."

It was a shocking indictment of the man Judy admired above anyone else in the profession. Ordinarily she would have made some angry reply and turned and indignantly walked back to the car. What stopped her in this shattering moment was the instant memory of the desperately ill Mrs. Pomeroy this afternoon. When she left the hospital, the woman's condition had still been a mystery, and perhaps worry about the patient had been nagging at the back of her mind all evening. Now she was linking Mrs. Pomeroy with those other cases John had mentioned and it frightened her to think what the outcome might be.

She said, "I have every faith in Dr. Holland." But it was more a bold front than a deep conviction; she was full of fear.

"So have I," he said with meaning, "in a healthy Dr. Holland. But suppose he is ill, ill and afraid to confide in anyone. I think I know what Bedford City Hospital means to him. And he must be aware of the uneasiness. The board and Dr. Granger and his clique are both breathing down his neck for different reasons. He knows to reveal any sign of weakness now will mean the loss of everything he's cared for over the years."

Judy stared at him with puzzled eyes.

There was a reminder of what she'd noticed in Dr. Holland in his study the other evening in the young man's face now. He spoke with the same feeling the old man had, and she somehow realized that in spite of the surface antagonism that apparently existed between the two, there was also a deep understanding on both their parts for each other. John showed that peculiar depth of feeling for the veteran surgeon that she had felt Dr. Holland showed for him. Yet, there was this cold anger separating them.

She said quietly, "You've made a strong case, Doctor. I can only hope you're wrong."

His eyes met hers. "You care a great deal for him, don't you?"

"Yes."

He shrugged. "Well, I won't hold that against you. In fact, I admire loyalty wherever I find it. But I thought I should tell you what I know. You're close to him. You may be able to approach him in this, help him in some way."

Judy realized her eyes were moist with tears. She said, "And you think this is why he didn't want you on the hospital staff. Because he thinks you know and may expose him?"

"It could go a long way to explain his attitude."

The awful part of it was Judy knew he was right. She looked down. "My head has started to ache terribly," she said. "I knew I was too tired to come out. Would you mind taking me home?"

"Of course not," he said, at once contrite. "I shouldn't have insisted on seeing you in the first place."

There was little said between them on the drive back. Judy's head was throbbing dully and she was filled with unhappiness by his revelation. She was almost certain his analysis of the situation was correct. She remembered the slight tremble she'd noticed in Dr. Holland's hand, the two occasions on which he'd faltered during surgery and the strange complications that Mrs. Pomeroy was suffering now after he had removed her gall bladder.

At last they pulled up in front of the house. John glanced at her with what seemed apprehension. "I hope I haven't lost your friendship tonight," he said unhappily. "I know you'll find it hard to believe, but I'm really eager to do the right thing."

She sighed. "If he is ill and in trouble, it isn't your fault. It would have happened whether you came to the hospital or not."

"You're still not convinced?"

"Not completely," she said. "Even if he

did have bad luck with those cases, it happens every day. He might even have trouble with another case and still only be having a run of special problems. I think I'll want further proof before I'll agree he's failing."

"How large a margin for error do you think he deserves?" There was a chiding note in his voice.

She managed a rueful smile for him. "I know you must think I'm terribly obstinate."

"I think you're wonderful," he said quietly. "I don't mind saying I envy your Dr. Holland. I wish you cared as much about me."

She was startled by the intensity of his words and he surprised her further when he reached over and gathered her in his arms. His lips found hers for a fervent kiss and he tightened his arms to bring her body breathlessly near his. She was weary and unhappy, but she had no will to resist. In fact, it was quite the opposite. She found herself wanting to remain in his arms. Here she felt some comfort from the nightmare that stalked her world.

When at last he let her go, he said, "I'm sorry I did that tonight. I should have waited. But I had to let you know how I felt, how I've felt since we met the other night."

She said, "What about Betty?"

"That isn't anything. I can hardly say we're even close friends. I've never been able to properly understand her, or she me for that matter!"

Judy studied him with a warm gleam in her brown eyes. "I wonder," she said.

"Wonder what?"

"If I feel the same way about you that you insist you do about me. It's strange, but you've been in my mind ever since the night of the benefit."

John reached out and took her hand. "I think we could know wonderful happiness together if everything isn't blasted by this mess at the hospital."

Judy's mood changed quickly. "Don't think it will make any difference if I do decide I care for you. Dr. Holland will still have my loyalty."

He smiled sadly. "Isn't that what I just said?"

This was the mood in which they parted. Even though she was weary and almost ill with worry she did not drop off into a sleep of exhaustion. Instead she lay for what seemed hours staring up into the darkness and wondering what the truth might be, the truth about Dr. Holland, the truth about John Randall and perhaps most important the truth about her own feelings!

It was raining the next morning when she drove to the hospital, and the nasty weather matched her own feeling of depression. She went directly to the operating room area and found a strange air of tension to greet her.

Jean Stephens, the circulating nurse, came to her with excitement apparent in her manner. "The schedule has been changed," she said. "The operation we were to do has been postponed until later and Dr. Holland and Dr. Small are doing an emergency on Mrs. Pomeroy."

"They decided that quickly enough," she said quietly.

Jean sighed. "I guess the Pomeroy woman is a lot worse. I hear they brought a special nurse in for her last night."

There was not much more time to talk. Dr. Holland and Miles arrived together and continued their grave discussion of the case as they went about scrubbing. Miles looked her way as if he longed to get her aside and talk, but they both knew this was impossible. Jean helped them into their gowns, masks and gloves. In the meantime, Dr. Bruce Hunter, an ambitious younger man who had recently taken studies to specialize as an anesthetist, was busy with the controls of the anesthesia machine.

Then the patient was wheeled in. Mrs. Pomeroy looked very ill and was already asleep from medication. Dr. Holland gave a great sigh as he stared down at her. Judy had never known him to react in this way before she raised her eyes to meet those of Miles across the table and saw the gravity of their expression. Dr. Hunter, calm and efficient, went about giving the patient a spinal block.

Then the operation started.

The tension she had felt when she arrived was heightened now. Once it came to her that in the smaller adjoining operating room John Randall must have already begun the ileostomy, but the demands of the surgeons beside her gave her no opportunity for wool-gathering. She had never seen Dr. Holland and Miles Small work better as a team.

With rapid incisions Dr. Holland cut through the skin and muscles. Soon the small bleeding that had occurred was taken care of by Miles, and Dr. Holland was probing in the area where they had worked before.

Suddenly he gave a quick glance at the anesthetist. "How is her heart doing?" he demanded anxiously.

"All right, now," Hunter sounded cautious. "Her pulse is 99."

"Scissors!" The command came from Dr. Holland in his familiar brisk operating room tone. She handed them to him.

"What do you make of that, Doctor?" It was Miles who spoke, sounding strangely uneasy.

"I'd say we had found the trouble," the senior surgeon said in quiet reply and continued working. "If you'll just help me here, Doctor."

Judy had no idea what they had found, but she could tell by the manner in which they spoke and the increased tempo of their activity they must have located the source of Mrs. Pomeroy's trouble.

At last Dr. Holland said, "That should take care of it, Miles." It was unusual for him to use the younger surgeon's first name when they were working at the table and it caused her to glance at him. Then she saw that Dr. Holland was swaying slightly. She was going to make some comment when Miles spoke for her.

"Anything wrong, Doctor?" he asked, urgency in his tone.

The old doctor raised a gloved hand to his temple in a weary gesture. "You take care of closing the incision, Miles," he said in a thick voice quite unlike his own, and he turned to cross slowly to the anteroom's swinging doors like a man groping through thick fog.

For a moment there was consternation in the group around the table. Young Dr. Hunter gave Miles a glance of frank alarm. Jean Stephens' eyes were questioning when Judy happened to turn the circulating nurse's way. This was something that had never happened before and none of them knew what to make of it.

"All right," Miles said, "let's proceed. It's only ten twenty-eight and that's not bad." He examined the walls of the incision for any bleeders. "Now we'll have our sewing instruction. The two-oh silk, Judy!"

With his cool assumption of authority, order returned to the team again. She handed him the thread and he went to work sewing the muscles together. He moved quickly and it seemed no time until he was drawing the merthiolate-painted skin of the incision closed.

As soon as Mrs. Pomeroy was wheeled out to the recovery room, Miles ripped his mask off and turned to face the members of the operating team. Judy saw that his handsome, aristocratic face had gone very pale and his eyes had taken on a cold gleam of authority.

"What happened here this morning was somewhat unusual," he said precisely. "I will depend on your professional discretion to say nothing to anyone about it. In the past there have been some regrettable incidents of loose talk and I don't want them repeated."

His announcement was met with a troubled silence. Judy could tell the others in the room were as much upset by the drama that had been played before them as she was.

Then Miles nodded to her. "Give me a hand with this gown, Judy." She rushed over to help him, knowing he meant it as an excuse to have a moment's privacy with her. As she fumbled with the gown he told her in a low voice, "It was a tied off gall bladder duct. The old man must have made the error when we had her on the table last time. Meet me at the cafeteria door at twelve sharp."

She nodded in silence and took the gown and gloves from him. He left the O.R. quickly as she turned to the task of supervising the room's cleaning. Miles had shocked her with his information. There could no longer be any doubt now that Dr. Holland was failing.

CHAPTER NINE

When she arrived at the entrance to the cafeteria, Miles was already there waiting for her. He led her by the arm and they joined the short line to fill their trays. She took very little and saw that he had selected a cheese sandwich and milk, which was scant fare compared to what he usually had for lunch. They headed for the table located in the rear corner of the room where they often sat because they could talk there freely without so much danger of passersby overhearing them.

As soon as they were seated, he said, "You may be interested to know Dr. Holland left the hospital right after he walked out on us this morning, and his secretary has no idea where he may have gone. Also, he has flight tickets booked for a late afternoon plane to New York."

Judy was aghast at these new developments. "What can it mean?"

"I have no idea," Miles said glumly.

"There's no doubt about your findings this morning?"

"None. A bile duct had been tied off. It

seems impossible that he could have made such an error. But there's no other answer."

She considered. "I can guess when it happened," she said. "You remember the spell he took at the operating table the day of Mrs. Pomeroy's first operation. It must have happened either before or after that — at a time when he wasn't himself."

Miles frowned. "I suppose the best thing to do is forget it. For this one error he's done thousands of perfect operations. It's not fair to make so much of it."

Judy's eyes met his gravely. "There is more to it than that, I'm afraid." She told him what Dr. John Randall had confided in her, the two other recent cases in which errors of a similar type had been made by the senior surgeon.

He gave a low whistle. "If Granger or any of his cronies hear that, the old man will be finished for sure!"

"I can't imagine why Dr. Holland didn't wait to talk with you."

"I fully expected him to," Miles said. "After all, he must have been very ill to have left as he did. For a moment I felt sure he was going to collapse. I intended to talk to him about his health and see that he had a proper checkup."

"He couldn't have wanted to face you," she said.

"That doesn't seem like the Dr. Holland we know."

"I'm beginning to feel you can't count on anyone," she said.

Miles let his eyes move toward the entrance door and with a wry smile he told her, "Here, at least, comes one hero who won't disappoint you."

She glanced around quickly to see he was referring to John Randall. There was an air of quiet dignity about the thickset young man as he joined the line with Dr. Staples. Both men were in what seemed a serious discussion of some topic and the diminutive Dr. Staples' hands were flying in accompaniment to his words.

Her cheeks flushed as she looked at Miles again. "I see he is with his prospective father-in-law," she said lightly.

The handsome face showed a sardonic smile. "I don't see Randall marrying Betty Staples, ever. For one thing, he's much too intelligent. They say he whipped through that ileostomy this morning like a veteran in spite of having Granger as anesthetist. Incidentally, Granger is acting as his chief press agent. He was already making the rounds of the hospital praising Randall as the new wonder boy of Bedford City's staff."

"I doubt if that will impress John much," she said.

Miles raised an eyebrow. "So it's John now?"

Again she felt embarrassed. "He's very nice. I don't think he likes too much formality."

"Apparently not," Miles said coolly as he watched the two doctors take a table some distance from them in the crowded room. Both men were still talking earnestly and paying no attention to their surroundings.

Changing the subject, she said, "Surely Dr. Holland will come back to the hospital before he leaves the city. If only to officially turn responsibility for things here over to you in his absence."

Miles shrugged. "He may or may not. I act for him automatically when he isn't here."

"Do you think Mrs. Pomeroy is going to be all right?"

"My guess is she'll make a fast recovery."

"Questions are going to be asked," she said. "I can just hear Head Nurse Raymond probing to learn what was really wrong."

"For the time being, you'll have to evade direct answers," he warned her. "Just tell her or anyone else who asks you there were unfortunate complications."

"Unfortunate is the proper word."

"Tragic would be better," Miles said, finally starting on his sandwich. "It is not pleasant to see a man coming to the end of his career. I think we're in on the sunset of Dr. Holland."

"I hope not," she said, although she was inclined to agree with him.

The rain continued and the balance of the day was as depressing as its start. For one thing, Dr. Holland did not return to the hospital. Judy learned from Miles that he had phoned and told the young doctor that urgent business was taking him to New York. He would be gone a few days and would appreciate Miles taking over as he always did.

There was a slight slowdown on the floor with two patients in the recovery room and no new ones entered. However, John's ulcer patient didn't seem to be responding to the medical treatment he'd planned for him and was giving quite a lot of trouble. As usual, Head Nurse Raymond resented this.

"You'd better go look in on him, Scott," she said with a scowl. "Mary doesn't seem to have any luck in settling him down."

Judy made her way down the corridor to the ulcer patient's room feeling she was being imposed on, but for Mary's sake she was willing to do what she could. The patient's name was Henry Webster and he owned an investment office with a real estate business on the side. He was reputed to be one of the wealthiest men in Bedford and John had been lucky to get him as a patient, or unlucky if you considered Webster from point of disposition. He was a big, irascible man with a shock of graying hair and coarse, pockmarked features. When Judy entered his room, which was the largest and most expensive on the floor, he was pacing up and down in pajamas with his dressing gown thrown on loosely. Both hands were pressed on his abdomen and he was groaning.

Seeing her enter, he paused to growl, "It's about time you got here!"

"What can I do for you?" was her polite stock opening.

"Nothing, I imagine," he said and uttered a small moan. "These pains are killing me and that whitewash stuff you're making me drink isn't doing any good. I want something to stop this suffering!"

"I'm sorry," she said. "Dr. Randall left strict orders as to what you are supposed to have."

Henry Webster faced her with his full fury

turned on. "I don't care two hoots for Dr. Randall and his ideas. I want some relief. I'd be better off in my own home. At least I wouldn't have youngsters like you trying to bully me around!"

"Yes, Mr. Webster," she agreed quietly.

He began to pace again. "I can't stay on here for days anyway. I told Randall that when I came in!" he said. "My time is valuable. My business needs me every minute. Have you any idea what I'm losing by staying here?"

Judy knew her reputation for outspokenness and the trouble it had brought her, but she couldn't refrain from saying, "If you gave us a little cooperation, you might lose your ulcers."

This caught him by surprise. He paused to glare at her. "You're a pretty nervy young woman!"

"So I've been told," she said. "But I hate to see you wasting your time and money, and that's what you're doing. Most of your present pain is probably brought on by tension. As long as you keep yourself in an angry mood it will continue. And you know what that will mean."

Henry Webster's pockmarked face showed concern. "What will it mean?"

"Getting along with a stomach about a

third the size of the one you have now," Judy told him calmly. "I've scrubbed for a lot of stomach ulcer operations and I can tell you they won't leave you much room to enjoy big steaks for a while. You'll eat small portions six times a day until you get your stomach distended to a proper size."

The big man looked actually frightened. "I've got no time to stop for meals a half-dozen times a day. I won't let Randall operate on me!"

"You'll have to if you don't give your stomach a chance to get better," she told him. "Either you try to calm yourself and keep on with the medicine or you give way to your nerves and let Randall wield his knife."

Henry Webster flinched at the word knife: "I want to get better," he said grudgingly.

Judy smiled politely at him. "Your next medication is in a quarter-hour. If you'll sit very quietly before and after you take it, I have an idea all those pains will disappear."

He hesitated a minute and then ran a hand through the straight-up, wiry gray hair. "Okay," he said, with a sigh. "I'll give your idea a try, but it better work!" He pointed a stocky finger at her.

She shook her head. "Uh-huh!" she protested. "That finger pointing set you back another minute. I want you to relax. Think of pleasant things."

Henry Webster slumped unhappily into the leather chair by the window. "What, for instance?"

Judy considered and shrugged. "Try dreaming about a big computer that would replace all your office employees and pick out all the winning stocks as well. Think of the money it would earn you." She left him with a thoughtful expression on his face.

That was the last crisis of the afternoon. The rain had eased somewhat as she left the hospital, but it was still drizzling enough for her to offer Mary Sullivan a drive home.

Mary's eyes were bright behind her glasses and her plain face was full of animation as she sat beside Judy in the car and described Dr. Randall's triumph of the morning.

"Everyone is talking about him," she said. "They think he's going to be another Dr. Holland and Bedford City was lucky to get him."

"I don't doubt that," Judy said, as she drove. "But don't you think the fact he is new tends to make them praise him a little more than is really justified?"

"Perhaps," Mary said doubtfully. "But he certainly is the hero of the hour now. And of course they're all saying the reason Dr. Holland is being to unpleasant to him is that he's jealous."

"That's ridiculous!" she protested, knowing her statement sounded a trifle hollow.

"Maybe," Mary said. "But he has given Dr. Randall a hard time. There must be some answer. That's what Dr. Granger says."

"If there is, you can be sure a gossip like Dr. Granger isn't going to come up with it," Judy said disgustedly.

After she had let her friend out of the car and resumed the drive to Redmond Acres, she felt a little guilty. Perhaps she had been too blunt with Mary, but hearing the stupid talk had annoyed her. If the people who started all the rumors worked half as hard as either Dr. Holland or John Randall, they wouldn't have time for such gossip.

At dinner, her brother-in-law brought up the fact that Dr. Holland had taken the afternoon flight to New York. "I was at the airport seeing a friend off when Dr. Holland went by on his way to the plane," he explained.

"I understand he had some business to look after in New York," Judy told him across the table. She had no intention of sharing the truth about what had happened at the hospital with either Moira or Paul.

Paul nodded. "It seemed to me he looked a lot older than when I saw him last. And he didn't recognize me. Went right by without speaking with one of those grim, preoccupied expressions on his face. I wondered if he might be sick, or if something had gone wrong at the hospital."

Judy managed a wan smile. "Not yet, at any rate. I do hear the board is out to cause him some headaches."

"They should leave him alone," her brother-in-law said hotly. "Holland is the hospital!"

Moira turned to her husband with a pretty pout. "That's hardly fair. Others do a great deal of the work. It will all be on Miles Small's shoulders while Dr. Holland is away."

Paul sat back and gave Judy a despairing smile. "I might have known it would end with Small getting a boast from Moira!"

It was still raining after dinner, and Judy decided to go upstairs and read for a while in her room before going to bed. She had just put her hand on the stair railing when the phone rang.

She answered it and it was John. He didn't sound as remote and shy as he had on the previous evening. "Surprised to hear from me so soon?" he asked.

"I guess not," she said, a hint of amusement in her voice.

"Good," he said. "I have a lot of things to talk to you about. Most of them can wait. What I am going to ask you this minute is, What about us?"

"I'm not sure that I've decided."

"You must have come to some conclusion," he pleaded.

"I think it would be nice to continue seeing each other."

"That's what I hoped you'd say," he said, sounding quite elated for him. "I don't suppose you're free tonight?"

"I'm free, but I'm dead tired," she said with a small laugh. "Tonight I'm going to bed early."

"Of course," he said, quickly reverting to his sober way. "And I'm having office hours tomorrow until all hours. Friday I'll be busy at St. Mary's in the evening." He paused. "How about the dance at the country club Saturday night?"

It was her turn to pause now. She knew that Miles sort of toot her Saturday nights for granted. Yet, she had not actually promised him to go to the dance this Saturday and he might not ask her. There were weeks they skipped. She made an impulsive decision and said, "Yes."

She knew it might start the gossips wagging their tongues lightly and Betty Staples might feel she was being neglected, but she didn't worry too much about those things. What she had not guessed was Randall's persuasiveness and that she would also spend Sunday afternoon and evening with him.

It was at dinner Sunday she told him, "Miles phoned yesterday and expected me to go to the dance with him last night. He was upset when I said I was going with you."

"Let him get used to the idea," he said with one of his rare smiles. "We have agreed we should see each other often. Remember?"

"I remember," she said. "He'll be furious when he hears we were together again today."

"Do you care so much?"

"He's a good friend," she reminded him.

John shrugged. "So after he gets used to the idea he'll still be your good friend." Then he changed the subject. "At least he won't be as busy as he has been the last few days. Dr. Holland got back this afternoon. I saw him for a moment at the hospital before I came by for you."

Judy was instantly on guard. She had not told John what had taken place in the operating room when Mrs. Pomeroy had gone through her second round of surgery and she didn't intend to. He had asked no questions and she had a shrewd suspicion he'd already guessed why the second operation had been required. Knowing how she felt about Dr. Holland, he had not pressed her for any details.

She pretended casualness. "Miles will be glad he's back. He doesn't enjoy taking on too much responsibility."

John looked at her with interest. "I imagine he feels that way because he is taking over for someone else. If the responsibility happened to be his own, he might feel differently. Judging by the appearance of Dr. Holland today, I'd say he might be asked to succeed him soon."

"Did he really look bad?" Judy was dismayed at the news.

"For the first time he seemed an old man first and the head of the hospital second," John said with a slight frown. "I only spoke to him for a moment, but my impression was that he was actually feeble."

Judy thought she knew why. The veteran surgeon had suffered a devastating blow in the discovery that he had made such a serious error in Mrs. Pomeroy's first operation. Even the fact that he had been able to correct it afterward would not make any difference to him. From now on he would be suspicious of his ability to operate, and for a surgeon of Dr. Holland's dedication, to cease operating was to cease living. Yet, all surgeons, regardless of their talent and fame, had to face up to this tragic reality one day. It seemed that Graham Holland's hour had come.

But he was to surprise them, and perhaps even himself, in the weeks ahead. Judy was surprised when he appeared at the hospital the next day with much of his old vitality apparent. She had expected to see the old man in bad shape from John's description of him on Sunday. It seemed the senior surgeon must have recuperated quickly with an overnight rest and now was ready to set a pace for everyone again.

The only one disappointed was Dr. Granger. He found solace in continuing to conduct his underhand campaign against the veteran head of the hospital, but Judy had a shrewd suspicion he wasn't getting anywhere. She had heard that Miles' father had taken the board to task for showing so little faith in Dr. Holland and this had silenced them for a while.

169

New patients were entered at the hospital and old ones went on their way. Dr. Randall continued to be a wonder. His skill at the operating table was fast becoming a legend and he confided in Judy that his private practice had grown by twenty-five per cent since his coming to join the staff of Bedford City Hospital. Perhaps the only person who showed small interest in the success of the young surgeon was Graham Holland.

The hospital head was now grudgingly civil to John, but he was not among those who touted his ability. The senior surgeon had cut down on his own schedule of operations and was passing more cases to Miles each week. Judy had scrubbed for Dr. Holland several times and on each occasion he had shown none of the physical weaknesses evidenced before. But she did note that he was wearing glasses in the O.R., and judging by their thickness, they must be extremely strong.

Her personal affairs were becoming something of a problem. Miles was not one to surrender her to a rival without a struggle, and although she had been spending most of her free time with John, Miles insisted on what he called the privilege of seeing her occasionally. This turned out to be fairly frequent. She had few evenings to herself.

She liked both young men but had even admitted to herself that it was John who was close to winning her heart. Miles was charming and fun to be with, but she couldn't visualize a lifetime with him. On the other hand, John was sober for the most part and certainly a lonely young man. He had been reluctant to discuss his background, but she gathered his home life had not been too happy although he came from a family that was not poor.

She had the feeling John needed someone to build his life around and believed that as his wife she might be able to help him find happiness he had obviously never known. While she had not committed herself, this was her feeling as the weeks went by. During this time there had been many changes at the hospital.

Calvin Ames had been discharged in an excellent frame of mind. He was still reporting for X-ray treatment as a normal safety precaution to make sure any of the cancer cells that might have escaped Dr. Holland's scalpel would be killed by radiation therapy. Every so often he made an appearance on the surgical floor to see old friends and offer words of encouragement to any new patients of his acquaintance.

Judy teased him, saying, "And you're the man who was so afraid of hospitals? Now we can't chase you away!"

He laughed, embarrassed. "I guess the place has come to play a big part in my life now. Fact is, I wouldn't likely have a life without it."

She hoped that the story would continue to have a happy ending and thought that the chances were good since they had caught Calvin Ames' lung cancer early. Mrs. Pomeroy had rallied quickly after her second operation and was now only a legend on the surgical floor. Their real problems with her had come as she convalesced and grew strong enough to walk about the corridors. It turned out that she had far too many obliging friends ready to smuggle in bottles of her favorite liquor, and in spite of all their efforts, she spent her last few days in their charge staggering about the corridors in various stages of intoxication.

However, she was cheerful enough and even planted a resounding kiss on Judy's cheek before she left. And promptly every Monday morning since her discharge a large bouquet arrived from the Pomeroy Floral Shop to grace Head Nurse Raymond's desk. Gallant Bess had been quite thrilled with this and made a lot of it until Miles had surveyed the flowers with a humorous twinkle in his eyes and dubbed them the most gorgeous rum blossoms he'd ever seen.

Gertrude Miller, the nervous little teacher, had emerged from her ileostomy operation quite a changed person. She showed signs of a sense of humor and regained her strength in a way that pleased both Dr. Randall and the nursing staff. With several weeks of summer still left to her, she would have plenty of time to rest and adjust to this new manner of living and be ready to begin teaching again when school opened in September.

"At least you won't be likely to get me back for an appendectomy," she joked with Judy as she waited for the elevator on the day of her discharge.

Judy found it hard to believe that the lively little woman was the same frightened person she'd talked to on the day she had come to the hospital. Henry Webster, John Randall's ulcer patient, had finally been discharged in an improved condition but far from cured.

Judy had twitted him as he left, saying, "You'll be back."

His pockmarked face took on a slow grin. "I'll wait until I get that computer that will take care of the office first."

The stream of patients continued to come and go. At home, Judy had been faced with a growing unpleasantness. Now that she was seeing more of John Randall, the light-hearted Miles Small had started dropping by the house on the excuse of hoping to catch her in. When he didn't, he seemed quite content to remain and pass a good part of the evening talking to Moira. This naturally upset Paul who still showed an un-healthy jealousy where Miles was con-cerned. Because of the circumstances, Judy felt some responsibility for what was hap-pening.

She had a startling reminder that other people were aware of the new closeness be-tween her and John when Dr. Holland sum-moned her to his private office one day. He wore a troubled look as he seated himself behind his desk to clasp his hands and study her a moment.

He began with, "What I have to say is strictly of a personal nature. I'd like you to think of me as your friend and not as head of the hospital."

She had no idea what he was leading up to, but smiled. "I do that in any case."

"Good," he said, nodding approval, and then as if he had real difficulty in getting out the words, he went on to add, "I want to speak to you about John Randall. It has come to my attention that you are seeing him a good deal."

Judy was astonished not only that he should have heard about their friendship, but that he should decide to mention it. She said, "What possible interest can it have for anyone?"

His weary face was grim. "I am interested because I'm worried about you. I think you should break this friendship with Randall."

"Why?"

"Purely personal reasons," the old man said. "You must have noticed that he has an odd personality. It is my feeling this will become a real problem as he grows older. I think he would be bound to eventually make you unhappy if you married him."

Judy was at a loss for words. "Why do you tell me this?"

"I'm basing it purely on what I know about him," the old man said. "Please don't ask me to explain beyond that." His eyes fixed on her with almost a pleading expression. "And please believe this to be the honest advice of an old man who cares a great deal for you."

She left his office with her head reeling. The entire interview still seemed like a bad dream to her. She couldn't accept Dr. Holland's warning as having any real validity. Yet, she knew by his troubled manner that he believed he had sufficient reason for talking to her as he had.

CHAPTER TEN

She said nothing to John or anyone else about her conversation with the senior surgeon. For one thing, she wanted to put it out of her mind and forget it like an unpleasant dream that had never happened, and also she knew whoever she told the story to would only put it down as another example of the change that had come over the head of the hospital. Rumors had simmered down for a while and she was not anxious to start the pot of conjectures boiling again.

Perhaps what Dr. Holland said had no influence on her directly, but afterward, she found herself sometimes regarding John Randall with new eyes. To offset his undoubted skill as a surgeon and his dedication to his patients, there was something distinctly cold and aloof in his make-up. He was sober at times when other men were light-hearted, serious more often than he was in a gay mood, and often obstinate when he merely intended to be determined. Because of what Dr. Holland had so earnestly told her, she became more aware of these shortcomings and worried that she might not be able to endure them in a marriage with the young surgeon.

Then something else occurred to throw her more in the company of the light-hearted Miles Small. It had all the trademarks of a French farce if it hadn't been so tragic. It was the sort of mess that only Moira could find herself in. The storm broke early one afternoon when Judy was called to the phone by a disapproving Head Nurse Raymond. The head nurse did not favor any of her nurses receiving private calls. As soon as Judy heard her sister sobbing at the other end of the line she knew something dreadful had happened.

"Come home as early as you can," Moira begged her. "I'm in terrible trouble."

"What is it?" Judy asked.

"I can't tell you on the phone, but please hurry. I'll be waiting for you." Moira had hung up with a loud last sob.

Judy drove home as soon as she was off duty and raced upstairs to the bedroom occupied by Moira and Paul to find her sister stretched out on her bed with her face buried in a pillow. Judy sat down by her and put a reassuring hand on her sister's shoulder.

"Now tell me what all this nonsense is

about!" she demanded, knowing at times like this it was necessary to adopt a stern attitude towards the lovely brunette.

Moira raised a tear-stained face to her. "Everything has gone wrong!" she declared.

"That covers a lot of territory," Judy observed grimly. "Are you speaking just for yourself or all the world?"

Moira sat up and touched a handkerchief to her upturned nose as she sniffed miserably. "You shouldn't make fun of me at a time like this," she said.

"I might not if you'd come to the point."

Moira wailed. "I don't know how! I'm so ashamed."

Judy gave a deep sigh. "This can go on for hours. Pretty soon you'll have me crying too and I won't even know why."

"It's Paul again!" Moira said angrily. "You know how unfair he can be."

Judy was not impressed. "Go on," she said.

"Well, he found some letters I was reading and went right up through the ceiling! Honestly, be acted like a crazy man!"

"What letters?"

"Love-letters," Moira said miserably, "from Miles Small."

Judy touched a hand to her temple and

groaned. "Oh, no! How could you be so stupid! And what is Miles thinking of!"

"Miles didn't send them to me lately," Moira explained hastily with the expression of a martyr. "He wrote them ages ago before Paul and I were married. They were so sweet I kept them."

"Moira!" Judy gave her pretty sister a scathing look. "I won't say you're crazy! That's too obvious! How did Paul come to find them?"

Moira was shamefaced. She kept wringing her handkerchief between her hands and staring down at it. "I had them out reading them the other day when the cleaner came to the door. I threw them in the dresser drawer instead of putting them away in the box in the closet where I'd been keeping them." She paused. "I guess I forgot I'd left them there. Today at noon Paul happened to be looking in the dresser and found them."

"Didn't you explain they were old letters?"

"I tried to," she said. "But he wouldn't listen. And there are no dates on the letters so he thinks Miles wrote them lately."

Judy knew how jealous Paul could be where Miles was concerned. In the face of this she couldn't imagine Moira keeping old love letters around but then Moira was capable of almost anything.

She said, "There must be some way of convincing him."

"Yes," Moira nodded eagerly, showing hope for the first time. "I think there is and you can help."

Judy got up and shook her head warily. "Don't try to involve me in this!"

"I have to," Moira said, standing also. "You're the only one who can save me. You see, the letters weren't addressed to me by name, just to *Dearest.* And I've told Paul that Miles sent the letters to you."

Judy's eyes opened wide. "You did what?"

"I had to!" Moira pleaded desperately. "You won't tell him the truth, will you? He half-believes it already and if you tell him it's so, he'll not doubt you."

"But I'm hardly seeing Miles these days," Judy protested angrily.

"You could go out with him more often," her sister said. "In fact, you should anyway. I don't like that moody Randall."

"Stop right there," Judy exclaimed, sinking on the other twin bed. "I have to put up with your framing me, but I'm not going to let you tell me what man I can go out with."

"Just back up my story," Moira said desperately. "Tell Paul the letters were sent to you and you gave them to me to read."

Judy rolled her eyes. "I suppose I'll have to but I'll hate myself for it!"

So Judy took the blame for the young surgeon's ardent love letters. Paul grudgingly accepted her word that the letters had been sent to her, but as a result of the mix-up, she began seeing Miles again.

Naturally this upset John Randall who voiced his resentment on a date they had one night in early September. They were sitting at a suitably isolated table in the dimly lighted coffee shop of the Bedford City Hotel.

Reaching out, he covered one of her hands with his. "You know that I am in love with you," he began.

"And I love you," she said with a faint smile.

"That was my understanding," he said, his serious eyes fixed on her intently. "It seemed we had everything settled. Now I am beginning to wonder."

"About what?"

"Why have you begun seeing so much of Miles Small again?"

It was impossible for her to tell him the rather long story involving Moira. The best she could do was put him off. She knew this

182

would not be easy and she began to wonder if she had been wise in thinking of marriage with him. He could turn out to be overly jealous like Paul. That was something she couldn't endure. Perhaps she would be better off to accept Miles.

"Miles is good company," she said, "and we're old friends. I don't think there's any harm in my seeing him now and then."

"Even though it makes me unhappy?" he said.

"I don't believe that it should. If you love me, you should trust me."

John sighed. "I trust you. But I happen to be a jealous person. And I know Miles Small still hopes to win you back. He is aware I've asked you to marry me but he won't accept it."

"I'm beginning to wonder if it would be a mistake," she said.

The young surgeon's sad eyes studied her. "So now we come to the cooling-off period."

"That's not fair, John," she said earnestly. "I'm worried for both of us. You as well as me. Marriage is a great step under any conditions and I'm not sure that we can get along together."

"We seem to have done well enough so far."

"That's different. Being together day after day, year after year, we might find we were not at all like the romantic pictures we've drawn of each other. For instance, there's your inclination to be deadly serious all the time. I think laughter has to be an important part of my life."

Randall sighed and absently toyed with his coffee cup. "I know I'm not always lively company. Let's say I haven't led the happiest of lives. Perhaps marriage and a wife with a lively sense of humor would alter me."

Judy offered him a perplexed smile. "I'd like to believe that. In fact, it's one of the reasons I became so fond of you. I thought you needed me and that has a surprising amount of meaning to a girl. Now I'm worried that you might resent my intrusions on your way of living and balk at any change."

"Have I shown myself to be all that hardheaded?"

"You're grimly determined," she said. "I can't properly explain it. But there's something out of balance in your make-up. I think the right wife for you could do something to make you more human. I don't mean more kind. You are very kind. And I've seen your tenderness with patients. But with all that, there is still a sort of barrier between you and other people. Generally you bring it down when you want to." She paused. "What worries me is that after we're married and I'm trying to help you in the way I think right, you'll shut that barrier down on me."

He considered this with an arched eyebrow. "It's a fair argument," he said. "You're attacking me in a vulnerable area. Yet, I know you're wrong and have no way of proving it."

"You don't have to prove me wrong," she said gently. "Give me a little more time to think about it and perhaps I may be as certain of our rightness for each other as you."

He shrugged. "I'm willing to give you all the time you want. But I'm not so certain I'm willing to share you meanwhile with Miles Small."

"Poor Miles!" she said with a faint smile. "Surely you like him."

"Not particularly," Randall said with a touch of the coldness that so often frightened her. "He has everything working for him, his money, his social position, his ex-governor father and the almost certain promise of succeeding Holland as hospital head."

"You yourself have said he's the one most

qualified for the job."

"That doesn't mean I have to approve of him personally," the young surgeon said with faint scorn. "At least I know where he lacks authority — at the operating table!"

Judy nodded slowly. "Yes," she said. "You're a much better surgeon, but sometimes I wonder if you're as good a man."

The rebuke almost made John flinch, instead he smiled coldly. "And, I suppose, that is what you must ultimately decide."

His goodnight kiss that night was no less ardent than on the many nights that had gone before. Judy trembled slightly in the embrace of his strong arms with the tender pressure of his lips on hers, trembled because she knew she both loved and feared this man. And long after she had seen him drive off into the darkness she pondered whether this combination of love and fear was what she should expect to feel.

The tempo at the hospital increased. A well-known Bedford trial lawyer, Patrick Lockary, was entered as a patient by Dr. Holland. Lockary was a tall, austere man with a lean face lined with years and character. Now in his late sixties, he was suffering from some form of gall bladder disorder and so had turned to Dr. Holland as a specialist. Judy had met the old lawyer at the country club and liked him. She wondered how his astute mind would react if he knew Dr. Holland's unhappy experiences at the operating table lately. Of course, the senior surgeon had been limiting himself to less difficult cases and operating only on certain days, so there had been no mishaps since the unfortunate blunder with Mrs. Pomeroy. At least, none she knew of. She tried to dismiss any worry about the lawyer from her mind.

He was in 441 and when his light came on Head Nurse Raymond gave her a nod and said, "He's your friend. See what he wants."

Judy left after giving Mary Sullivan, who was standing by also, a smile. They both knew the head nurse resented Judy's having friendships with some of the town's prominent citizens and never lost a chance to rub it in. When she entered the lawyer's room, she found him standing looking out the window. He was a gallant figure in his pajamas and colorful crimson dressing gown.

He turned, and seeing her, smiled. "I hoped they might send you down," he said. "To tell you the truth, I'm a little on edge waiting for all those tests Dr. Holland ordered, to begin." He spoke in a pleasant, deep voice that had charmed many hundreds of juries. "I admit to begin selfish and lonesome. I wanted someone to talk to for a moment. Does that shock you?"

She laughed. "Not at all."

"I've just gotten over a beautiful bout with my gall bladder," the lawyer told her. As he spoke, she studied him more closely and was aware of the sallow complexion so common to those with gall bladder disorders. "The worst feature of it," he said, "is these attacks always hit me when I'm working on a case."

"Probably because you're more careless with food then," she suggested.

"I've lived on snacks of hamburgers and french fries brought into the office day after day when I'm busy." He shook his head. "It looks as if I won't do it any more."

"You may not need an operation," Judy reassured him. "That is why Dr. Holland always takes very complete tests. He never resorts to surgery if there is a chance of a patient recovering without it."

"That's pleasant news," Patrick Lockary said with another of his warm smiles. "I thought all these fellows wanted to do was hack away at us."

"That's not true at all," she said.

The tall man looked more cheerful.

"Thank you, Miss Scott," he said. "I feel a lot better now. You've done your job well and I won't keep you any longer."

When she returned to the nurses' station Head Nurse Raymond gave her an inquiring glance. "What did 441 want?" she asked.

Judy thought a diplomatic reply was in order. "He had a kind of pain twinge," she told her, trusting this wasn't stretching the truth too far.

The face of the head nurse registered disgust. "Men!" she said. "Not one of them makes a decent patient!"

Judy made no attempt to argue the point with Gallant Bess. It would have done little good in any case since once the head nurse had made up her mind on any subject, she brought down the watertight doors of her brain and firmly shut out any new thought from trickling in.

Patrick Lockary was kept busy with the numerous tests and X-rays Dr. Holland had lined up for him, and in the late afternoon the head of the hospital came up to make his second round of surgical for the day. Judy had noticed he visited the various floors more often since he had started turning over a large part of his surgery to Miles.

She also noticed that the senior surgeon had taken to wearing glasses at all times.

This was a departure. She'd first noticed him with them in the O.R. Now he was using them, or a companion pair, even when going about the hospital. This led her to connect his eye condition with the errors he'd committed in surgery and she found herself worrying that he might be gradually losing his eyesight.

This afternoon he smiled at her and then went across to confer with Mrs. Raymond on the progress of Patrick Lockary's tests, after which he went down the corridor in the direction of the lawyer's room. At the same time, a light in one of the rooms near the lawyer suddenly went on and Judy hurried to answer it. That was how she came to be in the corridor a short distance behind the senior surgeon.

It was then something happened that shocked her and made her stop in her tracks. The old man walking ahead of her suddenly appeared to stumble and with a hasty, frantic movement, moved to the wall of the corridor and steadied himself against it. Judy watched with fear, undecided whether she should rush forward to him or wait to see what would happen next. She knew how sensitive he was about his condition and did not want to make it more difficult for him.

A surge of relief swept through her as she saw him straighten up and remove his hand from the wall. After a moment in which she could see him making the effort of pulling himself together, he resumed his journey down the long corridor. His step was not as resilient as before, but without witnessing his spell of a moment before, it would have been impossible to know what a grave condition he must be in.

Dr. Holland went on into 441 and Judy hurried forward again to look after the patient whose light had summoned her. But for the balance of the afternoon the memory of that moment in the corridor haunted her and she was filled with fresh concern for Dr. Holland.

Her depressed mood must have been clear on her face and in her manner for Moira approached her solicitously soon after she arrived home that afternoon. Judy had gone out to sit in one of the lawn chairs and read the evening paper when her sister came up to join her.

"You look terrible!" Moira said, sitting on the edge of her chair and studying her with anxious eyes.

Judy sighed and glanced up from the paper. "I have a headache," she said, which also happened to be true.

"You make me feel guilty," her sister said, her pretty face troubled. "I hope it hasn't anything to do with your seeing Miles."

"Nothing," Judy assured her. "I guess it's just that I'm tired. It's been a long, warm summer and I haven't had any vacation."

"You should take one, and soon," her sister advised.

"I've been thinking about it."

"Honestly!" Moira showed exasperation. She was wearing a smart blue cocktail dress and looking the epitome of an attractive young suburban matron. "I think you're ridiculous. You're much too interested in that job of yours and the hospital."

Judy smiled. "What's wrong with that?"

"I hate to see you make a slave of yourself," Moira protested. "I've been worrying about you anyway. I guess I've felt guilty ever since I made you go along with that lie."

"Don't think about it," Judy advised. "Paul accepted the story and I've been seeing Miles enough to satisfy him I was the one to whom the letters were sent."

"What about the other fellow?" Moira wanted to know. "I'll bet he doesn't like what you're doing."

"I'm not engaged to John Randall," she reminded her sister.

"But I think you would be right now if I hadn't upset everything," Moira insisted. "Sometimes I have a good mind to tell Paul the truth and he can take my word for it or not."

"You're already supposed to have told him the truth. Do you think he'd listen to a new version of your honest facts?"

Moira slumped back in the lawn chair with an unhappy expression marring her appearance. "I don't know what to do!" she said.

"In that case do nothing," Judy advised. "And as far as John Randall is concerned, you may have done me a favor. I was too ready to make an impulsive decision in his case. At least you've fixed it so I have plenty of time to think about what I want to do."

"You're probably just saying that to make me feel better," Moira said, but she looked a little happier.

It was a pleasantly warm afternoon for September and they were both still sitting outside enjoying the air when Paul arrived home for dinner. He came out to stand facing them, looking very much the neat young executive in his gray business suit and his short crew cut.

"Have you heard the big news?" he

193

asked Judy at once.

"What news?"

"Brandon Small collapsed downtown this afternoon, just in front of our store, as a matter of fact. They brought him inside until the ambulance arrived. Happened about four-fifteen."

She frowned. "No. I hadn't heard about it. I had left the hospital by then. I hope it isn't anything serious."

Paul shrugged. "I think it must have been bad enough. A lot of people were saying it was a heart attack, but you know how rumors get going. All I know is he was rushed to the hospital."

Judy was at once concerned for Miles' sake. And she was also worried about the hospital itself. If anything happened to Brandon Small, it would mean a change in the board. His had been its most important and stabilizing voice for years.

She got up at once. "I must go inside and call the hospital and see if I can find out what's wrong," she said. "I'm sure Miles will be there."

She made the call from the phone in the hallway and found out almost at once that Brandon Small was a patient on the surgical floor. She also learned that Miles was with his father and asked to be put in touch with him if he wasn't in the patient's room or occupied with his treatment. There was a long delay after that and much clicking of connections until at last Miles' agitated voice came on the line.

"Yes?" he said with a touch of irritation.

"It's Judy," she explained quickly. "I've just heard about your father. How is he?"

The young surgeon's tone changed at once. "Good of you to call, Judy," he said. "It's nothing too critical. He's had a touch of pancreatitis for some time and put off doing anything about it. Now there's a sign of internal hemorrhage. There's the question of abscess or tumor. It looks as if he'll have to have at least exploratory surgery."

"I'm glad it's no worse," Judy said. "There were rumors of a serious heart attack."

"I know," Miles said grimly. "There have been several frantic calls. But it's bad enough when you consider the tumor — and that's what his condition suggests — could be malignant. Dr. Holland is with him now."

"Good," Judy said. "I'll not keep you any longer. Let me hear from you when you have a moment." He promised he would and she hung up, a thoughtful expression on her face. She was wondering if Miles would allow Dr. Holland to operate on his father knowing his recent record in surgery. Also, whether she should warn him of what she had witnessed in the corridor only that afternoon.

CHAPTER ELEVEN

Head Nurse Raymond was in high good humor. The surgical floor was assuming an importance in the hospital of which she thoroughly approved. The fact that two of Bedford's most important citizens were patients there at the same time had caused it to become the focal point of staff attention. Also, the fact that Brandon Small was a member of the board and father of one of the hospital's staff surgeons gave him the status of a member of the family.

Judy was amused at the way the head nurse found excuses to drop by the ex-governor's room and there were no complaints about having to supervise his tests or those of the eminent lawyer, Patrick Lockary. Mrs. Raymond was determined to leave the two men with the impression the head nurse was a dedicated and tireless person and was playing her role of Gallant Bess to the hilt.

Judy had been looking after the lawyer and when she went to 441 and found it empty, she followed a hunch that he might have gone in to visit with his friend Brandon

Small. This proved to be a good guess. The tall lawyer was sitting in an easy chair by his friend's bed when she entered. At once he rose with a smile of greeting.

"I know it's time for my medicine," he said. "And I'm playing truant. But I had to find out how you were treating Brandon."

"No harm done," she assured him. "And do sit down. You're supposed to be ill. You can take your pills here just as well as in your own room." She passed him the pills and a small glass of water from her tray.

Mr. Lockary seated himself again with an amused expression as he took the pills and gulped down a mouthful of water. "That's what I like about it here," he told the other man, "the service is good."

The ex-governor managed a wan smile for Judy as well. He certainly looked ill and Judy had the impression he could be a very sick man indeed. His son's fears of a malignancy might be all too true.

"I agree," he said in a weak voice. There was a twinkle in his eyes in spite of his condition. "I must say the head nurse has shown herself to be most attentive and understanding and both my son and I agree Judy is charming."

The lawyer chuckled. "Of course, you have an advantage, Brandon; you've raised your own surgeon. Miles will probably do your operation free of charge."

The ex-governor shook his head. "I doubt that they encourage sons doing surgery on their fathers, do they, Judy?"

"No," she said. "I don't think you can count on Miles."

"Who needs him?" Lockary said grandly. "We have Graham Holland and they don't come any better."

"He's a fine surgeon," the man in the bed agreed. "And don't forget young Randall. From what I've heard, he's rapidly making a name for himself."

"John Randall is a good surgeon," Judy was quick to back up the elder Small's remark. It seemed to her it might be better for both men if they considered John for their surgery rather than the ailing Dr. Holland, but she could not express herself on that point here.

"And Judy knows," Small pointed out, "since she's often acted as a scrub nurse."

Judy left the two old friends still talking and went back to the nurses' station. She was worried about Brandon Small and the possibility that he might require a serious operation, for she now doubted Dr. Holland's ability to operate. She decided to tell Miles about the old man stumbling in the corridor on the previous afternoon as soon as she had an opportunity. But the opportunity would not come at the hospital it seemed. Whenever they talked, there was always someone else around.

Miles showed up on the surgical floor late in the morning and went directly to his father's room. Later he spoke to Judy at the nurses' station. "We should have all the tests done and the plates ready for study tomorrow," he said with a troubled expression on his face. "If we operate, it will be scheduled for first thing Monday."

She glanced up at him. "I have a few things I'd like to tell you," she said. "But I can't here."

"I'll be seeing you tomorrow night," he said with the first smile he'd shown since coming to the floor. "Remember, we have a date to dance at the country club."

Judy frowned. "Won't you want to come here?"

"I'll be here all through the day and early evening," he said. "I'm not going to rule out the dance unless Dad gets a lot worse."

"Whatever you say," Judy said. "I won't be angry if you cancel at the last minute. Please keep that in mind."

Miles gave her a knowing look. "Neither would John Randall. But don't think I will."

He stayed on the floor a few minutes longer and then left to go downstairs and see Dr. Holland. Noon came and Judy went to the cafeteria. It was not as crowded as usual and when she had filled her tray she found a table for herself. But she hadn't been sitting there long until a familiar serious-faced young man came by with a filled tray in his hands.

"Would a humble practitioner of medicine be welcome at this table?" John Randall asked with a faint smile.

"You're very welcome," she said. "And you are not a humble practitioner. Of course, you know that as well as I do."

John sat opposite her and began to arrange the items of food on his tray. "At least you must admit I get none of the eminent townspeople as patients," he said. "Or aren't you keeping a check on surgical?"

Judy smiled. "We've been far too busy."

"The score is very interesting," the young surgeon said. "Dr. Holland has the town's leading lawyer and an ex-governor, while to balance it, I have a sewerage worker, an insurance agent and an elderly retired school teacher. It is three to two but you must agree mine is not an illustrious list."

She gave him a reproving glance. "This is the John Randall I don't approve of sounding off," she said. "It seems to me that patients are all people and as individuals, important, regardless of their social position."

He cut into his open beef sandwich. "I would be the last to deny what you've said," he agreed. "But looking at it from another angle I don't rate the city's best people and I doubt that I ever will."

Judy shook her head. "Why must you be so coldly ambitious?"

"I merely would like recognition of my proven ability," he said. "I may not have Dr. Miles Small's charm and bedside manner, but aside from the great man, I'm the best scalpel wielder in this rather modest butchering establishment."

She smiled ruefully. "You're hopeless."

"And you prefer Miles."

"I didn't say that."

"You're going to the country club with him tomorrow night," John said.

"I've promised I'd go with you next week."

"Sharing plans never have appealed to me."

Judy's face crimsoned as she put down her glass of milk. "You have a knack for saying things that cheapen yourself and annoy me."

John regarded her in his sober way. "I'm a realist and I also think it's right to say what you think."

"You think such awful things!"

He said, "How does Miles feel about Dr. Holland operating on his father?"

Judy knew this was dangerous territory. She shrugged and very casually said, "I haven't discussed it with him."

"If I were in his shoes, I'd be worried," the young surgeon said.

"I don't even know that an operation will be required."

"I've just seen some of the plates they've taken in X-ray," John Randall said. "There's a growth involved. They'll have to operate."

Judy considered. "I didn't think they were certain yet."

"Probably because Dr. Holland hasn't seen those plates," he said. "You know, I find myself amused by this situation. I'm wondering if Miles will be willing to risk his father's life to sustain Holland's reputation. It would be a futile gesture since the old man is on his way downhill in any case."

Her temper flared. "How can you talk this way? Be so cold! And why do you hate Dr. Holland as you do?"

His eyes met hers. "Are you sure I hate him?"

"It shows," she said. "You can't conceal it. And it's not just professional jealousy or anything of that sort. It's something different I don't understand and can't explain."

The grave young surgeon chose to ignore her comment. Instead he asked, "Have you found out yet why Dr. Holland made his sudden unexpected trip to New York?"

Judy had almost forgotten about it. "No," she said. "I have no idea why he went and I don't think it's any of our business."

"I wonder," John said quietly, and as they rose from the table together, he added, "I enjoyed our lunch together."

She accepted the remark as another evidence of his tart tongue. Yet, a glance at the square, prematurely lined face of the young man suggested that he had really meant what he said. After they parted in the main lobby, she continued to think about him as she waited for the elevator. She had begun to think that the deep fondness she felt for him — call it love, perhaps — would not offset the pain his difficult disposition caused her. Many times she had seen divorce cases in which mental cruelty was listed as the reason for the breaking of a marriage and she saw that this could happen if she and John married.

Perhaps that was why Dr. Holland had even gone so far as deliberately talking to her about the matter. He had frankly warned her of John's bad disposition and the threat it offered to any enduring relationship with him. What really troubled her was the reason for John's being the sort of man he was. This cold bitterness was born of something buried deeply within him — some wrong, real or imagined — of which she had no knowledge. Perhaps, if she understood more about the factors that had shaped the young surgeon, she would be able to better judge the person he was now.

All his ability and quick intelligence was wasted in a large part because of his personality quirks. Once she had thought she might be able to change him. This could be possible if he wanted to be a different sort of person, but she didn't see that he did. The elevator came and she put aside her gloomy ramblings.

On Saturday evening, Judy was waiting when the familiar blue sedan rolled up in front of the house. "How is your father tonight?" she asked.

"Restless and having some pain," Miles

said. "We can't hold his surgery off much longer."

She knew the time had come to speak frankly to Miles. Staring at his handsome profile, she asked carefully, "Are you going to have Dr. Holland operate?"

Miles nodded. "I guess so. Dad seems to want him. I couldn't very well call Randall in on the case."

"I realize that," Judy said, watching the road ahead with worried eyes. "Yet, I wonder if you should have Dr. Holland. You know what has happened before."

"It's been better lately," he said. "I think he's been in reasonably good health since he took those few days' holiday in New York. It was probably just what he needed."

"What makes you think it was a holiday?"

Miles took his eyes from the road a moment to give her a puzzled glance. "What makes you think it wasn't?" he asked. "Actually, I've never asked him any questions about the trip."

"I wonder if he didn't go there to see a specialist of some sort. You must have noticed he began wearing glasses right afterward and now he's wearing them all the time."

"Lots of doctors wear glasses," Miles reminded her as they drove up the road to the club's parking area.

"I agree," she said. "But there is something else I think you should know." She told him what she had seen.

The alarm that showed in the young surgeon's face was very real and she was glad they had already arrived at the parking lot. He snapped on the safety brake and turned to her. "Why didn't you mention this before?"

"I didn't have a chance. Someone was always around."

"But this changes everything," Miles said. "If he really came that near to collapse, he certainly isn't in proper shape to operate on my father."

"I felt you were entitled to all the facts," she said. "I hope you know what to do about them."

Miles gave her no direct reply but took her into the main ballroom of the club where dancing had already begun. Crowds were slimmer with the passing of the peak summer weeks but the men in their white dinner jackets and black ties and the women in their gay dresses gave the Saturday night event a carnival air. Judy had worn her white dress again and tonight had used amber accessories.

Many people paused to question Miles

about his father, but they finally did get in some dancing, and when the music stopped, they found a table to themselves near the great glass windows overlooking the ocean.

Miles gave her a worried glance. "I've got to make a decision," he said, "and I think I've arrived at it. I am going to rush Dad to Boston tomorrow. They can still operate on him there by Tuesday."

Judy heartily approved of his idea. She said, "I think you are doing the right thing. But how will Dr. Holland feel if you do this?"

The young surgeon studied her grimly. "It seems I'll have to face him and have a proper showdown. The time for evading what we've all been able to see plainly has passed. I'll have to tell him that I no longer have enough confidence in him to allow him to operate on Dad."

"That is going to be difficult."

"You don't know how difficult," Miles said unhappily. "The old man has been just as much an idol for me as he has for you. Maybe I haven't been so honest in admitting it, but I can tell you now. If it wasn't my father's life at stake, I'd say nothing."

"Surely you can make it easier for him by suggesting there would be better facilities available in Boston," she suggested. "A more experienced operating team in that type of surgery."

"All that is true," Miles agreed.

"So you may as well use it in your argument with Dr. Holland," she said.

"The end result will be the same no matter what," Miles said. "I'm having Dad sent to Boston. I'll phone and make arrangements first thing in the morning."

Judy said, "Suppose your father doesn't want to go. After all, he is a board member and has a pride in the hospital. He believes Dr. Holland to still be the great surgeon he once was."

"I'll give him some story about his needing more than one expert on hand," Miles said, his handsome face wearing a tired look.

"And if he still doesn't want to leave Bedford?"

"I'll have no choice but to reveal the whole truth," he said harshly. "That Graham Holland is no longer competent."

There was a long silence between them. The orchestra began to play again, but neither of them was in the mood for dancing. They sat staring out at the ocean now blurred by the growing dusk, the tiny red and white lights of buoys and small craft standing out on its surface in vivid pinpoints. Judy knew that the young man opposite her was absorbed by the same unhappy thoughts that were troubling her.

At last she turned to him and said, "There's another face to this problem as well."

"Yes?" He spoke in a low voice.

"We have agreed that Dr. Holland shouldn't operate on your father. So that is settled. But what about the others, the average patients who are still coming to him and depending on his skill, the skill that is backed up by his position at the hospital. What about Patrick Lockary who is waiting to be operated on by him now?"

"What about them?" There was a new coldness in Miles' tone that shocked her.

She leaned forward, her brow furrowed. "Aren't you going to warn them?"

"How can I?"

"But don't you see it isn't fair!" she protested. "If Graham Holland isn't in a fit physical condition to operate on your father, he isn't well enough to be trusted with anyone else. Yet he has gone on operating week after week while we've known this truth."

Miles stared at her incredulously. "If you're asking me to expose him publicly, I can't do it. I'm not a Dr. Granger. I'll not stab a man in the back who has been like a father to me!"

"But you won't trust him to operate on one of your family," Judy argued.

"I'll not add that risk to the one that already exists," Miles said in an attempt to explain. "You know as well as I do that Dad in all probability has cancer. His chances are going to be slim. Knowing Dr. Holland may not be at his best, I can't send Dad into an operating room with him and perhaps eliminate even those slim chances."

"I know how you feel about your father," she said, "and I'm no more anxious to destroy Dr. Holland than you are."

"We owe him our loyalty, Judy," Miles argued. "You've always said that. I don't know why you've suddenly changed."

"Because I'm not sure any longer where our loyalties should lie," Judy said evenly. "Beyond our loyalty to Dr. Holland and the hospital, don't we owe some basic allegiance to our patients?"

He hesitated in answering. Then looking down at the table top, "I'd rather not consider it in that light, Judy."

"You think we should let things go on as they have been. Allow Dr. Holland to carry on as usual and make the same occasional unfortunate blunder that has been happening until he finally does actually collapse and the nightmare has ended."

"He hasn't had any trouble in the O.R. since he operated on Mrs. Pomeroy."

"Can you be so sure?" she asked. "John Randall says two cases came to him before that. Cases he referred to Boston. There may be others that we don't hear about because they don't return to the hospital! And some of them may have even died."

Miles stared at her helplessly. "All you're saying is pure supposition!"

"I saw him falter at the operating table on two different occasions," Judy told him. "Don't tell me that was supposition!"

He lifted a hand despairingly. "You're calling the questions, but you have no easy answer."

"I admit that," she said with a sigh.

Miles leaned forward, an intense expression on his face. "Give me a little time. Let me take care of my father first. I'll think about this in the next few days and I'm sure I can come up with some solution."

"You already have. By deferring the moment of truth."

"Holland has been sparing himself and doing well in the limited operations he's taken on lately. There's no harm in allowing him to continue as he is."

Judy shook her head. "I'm not sure that I'm able to agree with you, Miles."

She didn't change her mind. After he had taken her home and they had kissed goodnight she still worried about this touchy problem. She lay staring up into the darkness waiting for sleep and wondering what she should do.

CHAPTER TWELVE

Sunday was one of the perfect Fall days that come to offer a delightful extra to a summer just ended. Moira and Paul had gone to Providence to spend the day with friends and Judy was left on her own. She came down late and prepared breakfast dressed in green slacks and matching blouse. Her mind was on what was happening at the hospital and she was still filled with a confusion of doubts as to the best way to solve the problem presented by Dr. Holland.

She had just finished her second cup of coffee when the phone rang and it was John. "It's too nice a day to waste," he said. "How about coming out with me this afternoon and we'll have dinner somewhere."

Judy hesitated. She was not too eager to have to face the sometimes difficult young doctor in her upset state, yet she didn't relish the idea of spending the day and evening alone. And she knew Miles would be occupied with looking after the details of his father's transfer to a Boston hospital.

Deciding she would risk seeing John, she said, "All right. What time?"

"I doubt if I can manage it before four o'clock," he said.

"That's good," she told him. "It will give me plenty of time to be lazy before I dress."

And she did spend a couple of hours outside in one of the lawn chairs enjoying the unseasonably warm air and the afternoon sun. At three o'clock she came in to dress and by three-forty she was downstairs in a beige linen suit impatiently waiting for John to arrive. She heard the sound of a car coming up in front of the house, but when she went to the door, she was startled to see that it was Miles.

The young man got out and came nimbly up the stairs. She opened the door to him, knowing John would soon be showing up and not knowing quite what to say.

"I wasn't expecting you," she managed.

His expression was sardonic, as he said lightly, "Still, you are dressed in your best for someone."

She skipped that, though her cheeks warmed, and asked, "Why didn't you phone?"

"I did. But no one answered."

"I was out on the lawn," she remembered.

"It doesn't matter," he said. "I can only stay a few minutes. I wanted to bring you up-to-date on what's been happening."

"I've been frantic wondering," she admitted with a rueful smile.

Miles sighed and took a step forward then turned around. "I went to the hospital this morning hoping Dr. Holland might be there and he was. I was lucky enough to get him alone in his office."

"And?"

"I had a long talk with him. Told him I'd feel better if Dad went to one of the Boston hospitals specializing in intricate cancer operations."

"What was his reaction?"

Now for the first time she noticed how pale Miles was. He shrugged. "Not too good. Neither of us said the things we couldn't face saying. But I'm sure he knows why I'm doing this."

"What about your father?"

Miles looked grim. "He's too ill today to care what is done. In a way that's fortunate. I've hired a private ambulance and am going to Boston with him in an hour. There will be a room waiting for him. The operation is scheduled for Tuesday morning. I have permission from Dr. Holland to go up there again Tuesday morning and if all goes well, I'll return later in the same day."

"Well, at least you avoided any big

scene," she said quietly. "And that's what you wanted."

"I hope there's not too much talk. People like Granger will make the most of it, of course," Miles said unhappily. "But in the end no one will blame me."

She was about to reply when the doorbell rang and they both turned from where they were standing in the hallway to see the sober face of John Randall staring at them through the plain glass of the front door.

It was such a ridiculous situation, so like one of her sister Moira's mix-ups, that Judy laughed nervously. Then she opened the door. "Come in," she invited John. "Miles just dropped by for a moment to tell me about his father."

John raised an eyebrow but said nothing. He came inside and with a surly glance at Miles said, "Hello, Small, I hear your father is being taken to Boston."

Miles nodded uneasily. "Yes. It seemed the best idea. I'm going with him in the ambulance in twenty minutes or so."

Randall's serious face was thoughtful. "Have you a good man lined up?"

"Melanson at the Brigham," Miles said.

The other young surgeon's expression was approving. "The best," he said stiffly.

Miles turned to Judy. "Well, I'd better be

getting on. I'll let you know later how it all turns out."

"Please do," she said, seeing him to the door.

Miles turned back to John. "I'll be seeing you tomorrow, Doctor," he said.

John nodded. "You'll be coming back before your father's operation then?"

"I'll return Tuesday. Can't afford to lose a day."

"I understand," John said. He paused then added curtly, "Good luck!"

Miles acknowledged the wish with a nod and then was on his way out. Judy could almost feel the tension drain out of the room. She saw the blue sedan drive away and then gave her attention to John.

His usually serious face wore a grim smile. "Well, that was an interesting little get-together," he said.

"You can't blame Miles," she said. "He's very upset about his father."

"Obviously," John Randall observed dryly. "His father is a very important man."

Judy lost her patience with the sullen young man. "He's his father!" she said. "Surely you understand what the relationship means. Or do you?"

"Not too well," said with a wry smile. "What really intrigues me is how he got around Holland. It was an agreed fact at the hospital that Graham Holland would be doing the operation."

"Perhaps Dr. Holland was the one who suggested Boston," she said, not wanting to discuss any of this with the astute young surgeon when she was in such a state of confusion herself.

"You don't really believe that."

"What does it matter?" she said. "It's settled and that's all there is to it."

"You and Miles Small have been two of Dr. Holland's greatest supporters," he reminded her. "To have either of you turn against him must hit him where it hurts most. His pride!"

"But Miles hasn't turned against him!"

"Taking his father to Boston is an open admission he thinks Holland is no longer competent," John said, "and that's the way the hospital crowd will interpret it."

"Why do you take such satisfaction from that?" she asked wearily. "It breaks my heart to have Dr. Holland come to this. How can you be so cold?"

"Perhaps because I consider it a proper conclusion," he said with a shrug. Then, with another of his rare smiles, he said, "I don't think we'd better talk any more about it. It's an explosive situation at best and we'll never agree."

Judy sighed. "You get no argument on that. And you're right, it is time to enjoy a drive and some good food. Tomorrow we'll be back at the hospital facing it all again."

So they put aside their disagreements temporarily to enjoy the rest of the day. It turned out to be a good one. John found a quiet country road where traffic was light and the leaves already turning into a gorgeous array of colors. When they were tired of driving, they stopped at a pleasantly located roadside restaurant and spent their dinner period looking out over a small lake. By the time dusk came and they were heading back to Redmond Acres, Judy had forgotten most of the problems that had been plaguing her.

At the wheel, John said, "This has been one of our best days."

Settled back against the seat, she smiled at him. "Perhaps, because we both tried a little harder than usual."

"That's all we need generally do in life to make it better," he agreed. "And it's such a simple rule we forget it most of the time."

She stared out into the darkness as they drove along and thought that perhaps it would be possible after all. Perhaps she and John could marry and find the same kind of happiness they had known so briefly this afternoon. They had turned from their arguments and worries to enjoy themselves and they had succeeded better than possibly either of them had hoped. Could this sort of blissful truce exist between them for any long time? That was the question.

John must have been having the same thoughts, for when he kissed her goodnight, he said tenderly, "Let's try to hold on to what we found in each other today. Don't let me spoil it for us."

She went to sleep with his words repeating in her mind. And she knew a happiness that had not been hers before. John Randall had willingly admitted his weakness and asked her to help him. It was the first break in the surly young man's armor, the beginning for which she had waited so long.

Next morning, word passed like wildfire that Brandon Small had been whisked away to Boston in an ambulance the previous day. There were all sorts of conjectures, the one repeated most frequently being that the father of Miles Small was filled with cancer and his old friend, Graham Holland, couldn't face the hopeless misery of performing a useless operation. To spare him, Miles Small had transferred his father to a stranger's hands in Boston. Judy was glad the vivid imaginations had so quickly constructed a story to fit the circumstances. At least, it would spare Dr. Holland for a while.

She had been waiting with some apprehension for her first meeting with him on Monday morning. She couldn't help wondering if he would show signs of the realization that must have come to him as a result of losing Brandon Small as a patient, and she worried that the old surgeon might see her own doubt of him plainly mirrored on her face.

As it turned out, the events surrounding their meeting came about in a way much different from her imagining. She was in the room with Patrick Lockary giving him his regular medication when the senior surgeon came into the room. A glance at his ashen face told Judy that the old man fully understood his own position, but he seemed determined to play out his bluff gallantly.

"Your plates have come at last," he told Lockary with a ghost of a smile. "I must say I'm not satisfied. I am almost sure we have stone blockage but the plates show no shadow."

The tall lawyer gave the old man a questioning look. "So what does that mean?"

Dr. Holland shrugged, the bulldog face showing frustration. "I've got you down for surgery on Wednesday morning," he said. "We'll have to explore and see if we can find something that isn't showing on the plate."

"I see," the lawyer said with a wry smile. "Sort of like traveling without a map."

"Not quite that serious," Dr. Holland said, and he drew the plates out of the brown envelope in which he was carrying them and held them to the light for Lockary to study them himself. "You can see they are quite clear."

The lawyer sighed. "I'm afraid I'm not qualified to offer an opinion. But quote me any legal problem and I'll be able to oblige."

"We'll not worry too much," Dr. Holland said, putting the plates back in their envelope and putting the envelope on the bed for a moment.

"I hear they've taken Brandon Small to Boston," Lockary said.

"Yes," the surgeon said with a sigh.

The lawyer's pleasant face showed concern. "Was he all that bad? It was understood you were to do the operation here."

Dr. Holland raised a protesting hand. "It is a matter on which I'd rather not offer an opinion at this moment." His heavily lined face was purplish as he turned to Judy. "Keep a close check on the patient, Miss Scott. I'll continue to look for a detailed report each day." Without saying anything more to Patrick Lockary, he strode out of the room.

The tall lawyer gave a speculative whistle as the door closed after the old doctor. "He's not himself today," he said. "This business of sending Brandon Small to Boston seems to have upset him badly."

"I'm afraid so," she agreed, gathering her things on the tray and ready to leave. Then she noticed the doctor had gone out and left the envelope with the plates on the bed. "He forgot these," she said, holding them up.

"So he did!" Patrick Lockary said frowning. "Pictures of my enemy, Miss Scott. I couldn't make anything of them. Can you read plates?"

"I've taken quite a bit of training in it," she admitted.

The tall man brightened. "Excellent!" he said. "Let's hold them up to the window again and you can explain them to me."

It seemed a small enough favor to satisfy the lawyer so she took the plates from the envelope and went to the window to hold them against the sunshine streaming in. Lockary came to stand beside her and listen gravely while she explained the details of the plates. It was when she held up the second one that she gave a small gasp.

The lawyer glanced at her in alarm.

"What's wrong? You were just making the guided tour interesting. Find something bad?"

Quickly regaining her poise, she said, "No. But I should get these back to Dr. Holland. He'll be worried about them." She excused herself and left.

But it wasn't Dr. Holland she sought out first. Instead, she went directly to John's office. She was lucky to find him seated at his desk. His square face showed surprise as she came hurrying in to him.

"You look upset," he said, rising. "Something new happened?"

"I need your opinion," she told him, already sliding the plates from the brown envelope. "What do you make of these?"

He rose, examined the plates and then glanced at her. "Simple case of blockage from gall stones. It shows very clearly on nearly all the plates."

Judy sank into the chair by his desk. Looking up at him, she explained, "Those are Patrick Lockary's plates. Dr. Holland had them in his room just now and said he couldn't find any clue to what was wrong from the plates."

"But it's too plain to miss!"

"For us to miss," Judy said meaningfully. "Dr. Holland has been complaining about fuzzy X-ray plates for weeks when there has been nothing wrong with them." She paused. "What will I do?"

An ironic smile crossed the young surgeon's face as he returned the plates to the brown envelope and placed it on the edge of his desk. Then he went around to sit in his chair again.

"I wish you'd be as quick to come to me for advice in other matters," he said. She knew he was referring to her seeing Miles and the quarrel that had resulted from it.

She pleaded, "Can't we keep this above a personal level? This concerns the hospital and the future of someone who means a great deal to us."

"All right," John said at last, "I think we should forget what you have seen. It is not your business. Give the plates back to Dr. Holland and say nothing to him or anyone else."

"You can't be serious!"

His voice was quietly even. He said, "I am completely serious. He is capable of discovering his own mistakes. You owe it to him to let him do that."

Judy was leaning forward in her chair, incredulity on her pretty face. "But he didn't find out in time with those other patients. How can I be sure he will now?"

"You have no right to question him!"

Judy got up. "I owe something to my patient."

"Dr. Holland's patient!" John said sharply. "I think you are forgetting your position in all this."

"You expect me to let him blunder on and perhaps make some terrible error when he's operating on Patrick Lockary!"

"That is hardly likely to happen."

"It has before," she said. She was startled and confused at John's attitude. She had been certain he would join with her in pointing out Dr. Holland's error to him and helping her ease the delicate situation. Instead, he was asking her to ignore what had happened altogether.

He shrugged. "You are the one who came here for advice," he said. "Yet, you don't seem eager to take it."

"I'm sorry," she said, "I shouldn't have troubled you." She picked up the envelope and started for the door.

John was right behind her, a restraining hand grasping her arm. "Wait!" he said in an urgent tone.

She hesitated and glanced at him with troubled eyes. She saw that he was deeply concerned, his expression showing both frustration and unhappiness.

"I'm going to ask you to change your mind about facing Dr. Holland with these," he said. "For our sake, if for no other reason."

Judy tried to fathom the meaning of the tortured look in his hazel eyes. "It's no use, John," she said. "Please let me go!"

He released his grip on her. "Let me warn you, then," he said. "I'm not sure I'll be able to forgive you if you do this against my wishes."

Long after she left his office, the memory of his words tortured her as they echoed through her mind. She moved slowly along the wide corridor deliberating on what her next move must be. John had shocked her with his strange, unrelenting decision that she should not expose the senior surgeon nor even confront him with his error. But all her own training and principles made it impossible for her to condone this wrong. The kindly, lined face of Patrick Lockary haunted her. She knew the old lawyer trusted her along with the others and she would not let him down.

Nearing Dr. Holland's office, she realized what she was about to do could finish her with John. It could mean the end of their love. He was capable of any coldness once his mind was made up. If he wanted to believe her wrong in this, she had no doubt he would turn from her. It could also mean the loss of her job as Dr. Holland might see fit to dismiss her. What should she do?

She was at the door of the senior surgeon's office and she knew there had never been any choice for her. The old man was on the phone and when he finished his call, she offered him the brown envelope.

"The X-ray plates," she said. "You forgot them."

He took them and put them to one side. "Thanks," he said. "I missed them."

"There is something else I must tell you, Doctor," she said, a tremor in her voice but her courage high now that she had embarked on a course. "These X-rays show a gall bladder obstruction clearly. I don't know how you missed their message. I can only believe it is because you are no longer yourself."

"Is that all you have to say, Miss Scott?" the old man's voice had a sharp edge.

"You know why Miles Small rushed his father to Boston. Because he knew you were not well enough to do the operation. Isn't it about time you admitted to the truth about your condition? Before you do any more harm?"

The old man had risen and was standing

with his head high and his rugged old face grim. "You have said quite enough, Miss Scott," he told her. "You may go now."

She left his office in a fog and remained in one all the rest of the afternoon. Somehow, she got through her work and managed to make answers to any questions put to her. At last she came to the end of her shift and went home. There she spoke vaguely of a headache and kept upstairs by herself away from Moira and Paul. All during the evening she hoped that a phone call might come from John. But the young surgeon apparently had meant what he said. He was not going to forgive her for confronting Dr. Holland with his error. No call came!

Judy was convinced this might end her career at Bedford City Hospital, and nothing happened to change her mind when she reported for work the next morning. It was ten o'clock when Head Nurse Raymond summoned her to the nurses' station and told her, "Dr. Holland wants to see you in his office right away."

She took the elevator downstairs feeling that the moment of crisis had come at last and feeling too sick about the whole business to care. When she entered the old man's office, her first surprise was finding John Randall standing there. There was nothing in his expression to hint that he had relented in his attitude, but as Dr. Holland guided her to a chair, she sensed the old man's manner was much different from the previous day.

Then, with John standing by soberly, Dr. Holland addressed her across his desk. "I know what you did yesterday was out of high regard for me and I want you to believe that I fully appreciate it. You are the only one who had the courage to stand before me and say what you did. I should have stopped operating months ago. It began with headaches, moments when my vision blurred. I went to a leading man in New York and I received a verdict only yesterday. I have a brain tumor. I'm going for an operation next week." The old man smiled wearily. "So you see you were right to bring me to task. I understand Dr. Randall was against your doing so. I must say he's the last one I'd have expected sympathy from."

Judy sighed. "I'm sure Dr. Randall has a deep respect for you and meant well. I'm sorry I had to oppose him in this. I think he should be the one to operate on Patrick Lockary. I know he'll measure up to your standards in the O.R."

A faint twinkle showed in the veteran doctor's eyes. "I hope so," he said, "since John

Randall happens to be my son." He gave the young man a smiling glance with the ordinarily sober John beaming back at him happily.

Judy could never be certain what went on in the first few moments after this surprise. She only knew that Dr. Holland excused himself on some pretext and she found herself alone in the private office with his son.

John Holland took her in his arms, "This time I'm the one who's asking for advice," he said. "How can I expect you to forgive me?"

"That's not difficult at all," she said softly. "You have a charm that's hard to resist, Doctor."

After he kissed her and asked her again to marry him, he went on to explain, and it was then she realized the meaning of the duel between the old doctor and his talented son. It was the story of Dr. Holland's estranged wife who had raised her son under her maiden name and planted a hatred for his father in him. On her death, his desperate emotional need had brought John Holland to Bedford to find out the sort of man his father really was.

Patrick Lockary was operated on the next morning and his operation was successful. Miles returned from Boston with good news about his father as well. It was at the end of a week in which Judy thought almost everything that could happen had happened, yet there was still another surprise in store for her. The one to offer it was a proud Moira when Judy went home Friday evening.

"Guess what?" her pretty sister said excitedly. "You're going to be an aunt!"

Judy didn't quite realize for a moment. Then she gasped. "You and Paul! At last! When did you find out?"

"Today," Moira said. "I mean, I found out for sure today. So Paul shouldn't be jealous anymore even if you don't marry Miles Small. And you aren't going to, are you?"

She smiled sadly. "No, Moira. I'm not going to."

"I knew you wouldn't after that John Holland started coming here," Moira said with a sigh. "Of course, he won't make you anything like as good a husband as Miles Small would have, but I will admit all the girls in town think he's something."

Judy eyed her sharply. "It sounds like Paul has new worries. I'd better keep my eye on you."

"Oh, I wouldn't flirt with John," Moira said, blushing. "I'm going to be a mother. And anyway, if I have any spare time for anyone, it will be poor Miles!"

"I think it's time poor Miles found himself a girl of his own," Judy said firmly. "And I have an idea he will."

It turned out she was right. A pert redhead in therapy caught the tall young man's attention almost as soon as he came back from Boston. And since she came from a prominent family in Connecticut and had the same gay sense of humor that he did, they made a wonderful couple.

Dr. Graham Holland's stay in New York was not a short one. His condition required two operations rather than one, but they were successful and the old man had been assured he could return to Bedford and his position as head of the hospital if he did not push himself too hard. Meanwhile, a long convalescence lay ahead of him.

It was for this reason that John and Judy were married in the Little Church Around the Corner in New York. It was a simple affair with just the officiating clergyman and witnesses, but it was all that Judy wanted. The reunion with his father had done a great deal to make John a more balanced person. And so it was natural that after the ceremony the first place they went was the uptown hospital where Graham Holland was still convalescing.

Propped up against pillows, his head still bandaged, the old man greeted them with a smile. "The big moment for me at weddings," he said, "always comes when the bride and groom kiss." He winked for Judy's benefit. "Of course, I missed your ceremony but maybe you'll repeat the kiss for me now." They did.

We hope you have enjoyed this Large Print book. Other Thorndike, Wheeler or Chivers Press Large Print books are available at your library or directly from the publishers.

For more information about current and upcoming titles, please call or write, without obligation, to:

Publisher
Thorndike Press
295 Kennedy Memorial Drive
Waterville, ME   04901
Tel. (800) 223-1244

Or visit our Web site at:
www.thomson.com/thorndike
www.thomson.com/wheeler

OR

Chivers Large Print
published by BBC Audiobooks Ltd
St James House, The Square
Lower Bristol Road
Bath BA2 3BH
England
Tel. +44(0) 800 136919
email: bbcaudiobooks@bbc.co.uk
www.bbcaudiobooks.co.uk

All our Large Print titles are designed for easy reading, and all our books are made to last.